AM

"Thank you for coming after me, Rafiq."

His eyes flashed violently. He gripped her hands so fast and tightly she dropped the jar of ointment.

"Paige." His voice was rough, low. "I will get you out. I promise you that. On my life."

She swallowed, suddenly unable to speak. The passion and ferocity in his grip, the brilliance in his eyes wrapped around her, flowed through her, sparked a hot thrill deep in her belly.

He pulled her to him. Shock and heat rippled through her as his lips moved over hers, hard, hungry, possessive.

A loud banging sounded on the door and he pulled back, his eyes flashing, breathing ragged. "Paige—" he touched her cheek "—before everything changes…" His eyes bored into hers. "No matter what happens, I *will* keep you safe. Believe in me."

Dear Reader,

What better way to keep warm on these brisk November nights than being caught up in the four adrenaline-pumping romances Silhouette Intimate Moments has for you!

USA TODAY bestselling author Merline Lovelace starts off the month with *Closer Encounters* (#1439), the latest installment in her CODE NAME: DANGER miniseries. An undercover agent and a former D.A. must work together, all while fighting a consuming attraction, to solve a sixty-year-old murder. RITA® Award-winning author Catherine Mann continues her WINGMEN WARRIORS series with *Fully Engaged* (#1440). To save a woman from his past, an Air Force warrior must face his worst nightmares.

Popular author Cindy Dees delights us with *The Lost Prince* (#1441), where a Red Cross aide must risk her life and her heart to help an overthrown prince save his crumbling nation. And be sure to read *A Sultan's Ransom* (#1442), the second book in Loreth Anne White's SHADOW SOLDIERS trilogy. Here, a mercenary and a doctor must team up to stop a deadly biological plague from wreaking havoc on the world.

Over the next few months, watch as Silhouette Intimate Moments brings exciting changes to its covers, and look for our new name, Silhouette Romantic Suspense, coming in February 2007. As always, we'll deliver on our promise of breathtaking romance set against a backdrop of suspense. Have a wonderful November, and happy reading!

Sincerely,

Patience Smith
Associate Senior Editor

Please address questions and book requests to:
Silhouette Reader Service
U.S.: 3010 Walden Ave., P.O. Box 1325, Buffalo, NY 14269
Canadian: P.O. Box 609, Fort Erie, Ont. L2A 5X3

Loreth Anne White

A SULTAN'S RANSOM

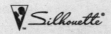

Silhouette®

INTIMATE MOMENTS™

Published by Silhouette Books

America's Publisher of Contemporary Romance

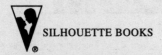 SILHOUETTE BOOKS

ISBN-13: 978-0-373-27512-0
ISBN-10: 0-373-27512-9

A SULTAN'S RANSOM

Copyright © 2006 by Loreth Beswetherick

Visit Silhouette Books at www.eHarlequin.com

Printed in U.S.A.

Books by Loreth Anne White

Silhouette Intimate Moments

Melting the Ice #1254
Safe Passage #1326
The Sheik Who Loved Me #1368
*The Heart of a Mercenary #1438
*A Sultan's Ransom #1442

*Shadow Soldiers

LORETH ANNE WHITE

As a child in Africa, when asked what she wanted to be when she grew up, Loreth said a spy…or a psychologist, or maybe marine biologist, archaeologist or lawyer. Instead she fell in love, traveled the world and had a baby. When she looked up again she was back in Africa, writing and editing news and features for a large chain of community newspapers. But those childhood dreams never died. It took another decade, another baby and a move across continents before the lightbulb finally went on. She didn't *have* to grow up. She could be them all—the spy, the psychologist and all the rest—through her characters. She sat down to pen her first novel…and fell in love.

She currently lives with her husband, two daughters and their cats in a ski resort in the rugged Coast Mountains of British Columbia, where there is no shortage of inspiration for larger-than-life characters and adventure.

To Jo for her tireless support and inspiration.
To Irene for hauling me out onto the trails
for much-needed breaks.

And as always, to my wise and wonderful editor,
Susan Litman.

Chapter 1

Stars glittered in the vast Arabian sky, giving Rafiq Zayed just enough light to work without night scopes. Flint chinked against his shovel as he scraped sand from beneath the electrified perimeter fence that guarded the 12,000-acre laboratory compound.

The night had cooled, but he could smell the residual warmth of the day's sun trapped in the deeper layers of desert sand. He could feel it rise softly against the skin he'd left exposed around his eyes. The rest of his face was hidden by a black turban he'd wound around his head, Bedouin-style. The camel he'd hobbled behind him snorted softly as it tugged at sparse tufts of dead grass.

A dog barked suddenly in the distance.

Rafiq stilled, listened. Waited.

A car door slammed somewhere and an engine started, the sound gradually dying into the distance. Then all was quiet again—that expansive hush peculiar to the desert, marred only by the distant murmur of ocean waves against sandstone cliffs.

He quickly secured the shovel to his camel bag, ready to refill the hole on his return. He could leave no sign that he had ever been here. The slightest mistake would alert the enemy and instantly trigger a biological attack on the United States. Millions would fall ill within hours, and then the violence would spread—people killing each other in a wave of pure murderous terror.

And it would only be a precursor, the first in a series of events designed to topple the U.S. government and seize control of the global economy.

He narrowed his eyes as he studied the massive black Nexus Research and Development Corporation laboratory complex in the distance. The antidote, the answer to it all, lay somewhere in those buildings in this secure U.S. corporate compound on Hamānian soil. He'd memorized the layout from blueprints secured from the French construction company that had built the place. He needed to get into the fourth quadrant on the left.

He squashed himself flat, wriggled through the hole. Once on the other side, he dusted sand from his tunic and consulted his watch. The soft green glow showed he had about three hours of complete darkness left, max.

He hunkered down and ran low over the sand, his hand primed to grasp the *jambiya* at his waist at the slightest sign of movement in the night shadows.

* * *

Dr. Paige Sterling worked with customary slow and calculated movements, air hissing gently through the yellow hose that plugged into the back of her bright blue biohazard suit. The inside of her suit smelled faintly like the inside of a new plastic bucket, and her flexible helmet restricted her peripheral vision. But she was in her comfort zone—the Biosafety Level 4 lab where she routinely handled pathogens for which there was no known cure. Here, no task could be rushed. Every action had to be measured, because one slip would mean death.

This was her kind of science, gut-checking, high-stakes work that required a level head and laser focus at all times. This is where Paige did preemptive research that she hoped would help save lives one day, and it took a particular personality to work regularly in maximum containment like this, an ability that far exceeded mere scientific competence. Paige prided herself in being such a personality, and her knack for maintaining her cool in the hot zone was a trait she carried well beyond the lab and into her personal life.

She picked up the vial she'd taken from the cryogenic container that had arrived in the shipment room early that morning and lumbered over to the stainless steel lab table in her heavy yellow boots. She held the vial up to the light. It was labeled simply with a bar code that meant nothing to her. But it was the contents of the glass tube that piqued her interest.

This sample had arrived early this morning in a biohazard container from the Ishonga region of The Republic of the Congo and had been destined for Quadrant 3, *not* for her quadrant. This had puzzled her.

Her disease—her exclusive research project—had its

origins among a unique and elusive troop of bonobos that resided only in the remote Blacklands region near Ishonga. It was work her parents had started, and the Blacklands was where her parents had vanished 17 years ago. The unsolved mystery of their disappearance was something that haunted Paige, and *nothing* ate at Paige Sterling like an unanswered question—which was why she'd taken the sample against her better judgment.

"Curiosity killed the cat, Paige," she muttered as she emptied the biological sample onto a cutting tray. She selected a scalpel and began to slice tiny bits of tissue into the size of pinheads. Paige worked meticulously, taking care not to puncture the latex gloves she had taped to her sleeves. The sample had been marked Biohazard Level 4. She had no idea why—and she wasn't taking any chances.

She reached for an empty test tube in the rack to her right…and sensed sudden movement behind her.

She froze.

Someone was in her office, on the other side of the thick glass pane that separated it from her lab. Paige turned her upper body very slowly, enabling a view round the side of her visor. But she could see nothing.

A whisper of nerves died in the hiss of her suit. She shook herself. The lab compound was secure. There were guards, electrified fences, pass codes, video surveillance in the corridors. It was almost two in the morning. No one *could* be in here now, apart from the bonobos in the cages in the next room. Her pygmy chimps always seemed to sense her presence and get excited. Perhaps she'd just sensed *them* this time.

But she couldn't quite shake the unease that murmured through her. And that in itself unsettled Paige. She *never* felt skittish in her lab. She couldn't afford to. She told herself it was just guilt at having "borrowed" one of the samples that had been shipped into the Nexus compound early this morning.

She forced her attention back to her task, telling herself it was probably just some other disease from the same region that Quadrant 3 was researching. But deep down she knew this was unlikely. She dropped the samples into the test tube and filled it with a fast-drying plastic resin that penetrated and hardened the tissue almost immediately. She removed the now-hard cylinder of tissue and lumbered carefully over to the ultramicrotome, a diamond-bladed, tissue-slicing machine that produced ultrathin sections. She shaved the cylinder into minute rounds, placed them onto a copper sample screen and dropped the screen into the electron microscope holder.

Paige steadied herself with two deep breaths, then seated herself at the microscope station, mindful of the hose connection in the back of her suit. She adjusted the dials and peered into the microscope, allowing her gaze to relax as she entered life at the cellular level—her world. But as she began to move through thread-like neurons and pods of coiled proteins, her heart skipped a beat. Her fingers tightened on the dial. She zoomed in, and everything leaped to higher magnification. An unspecified fear began to leak through her veins.

This couldn't be true.

She zoomed to an even higher magnification, the images pouncing out at her. And her heart began to thud. There was no mistake. This was *human* brain tissue, and it was riddled with holes like a sponge. It also had the distinctive prions— malformed proteins—that were the biological signature of *her* recombinant pathogens, diseases that were *not* supposed to exist beyond the walls of this lab. Diseases that, until now, she had only seen manifested in her primate trial groups.

Never in humans.

Paige tried to swallow against the tightness in her throat. She had no idea what went on in Quadrant 3, just as the scientists in Q3 should have no knowledge of her work in Q4. Keeping the various quadrants compartmentalized was the Nexus way of guarding highly sensitive and incredibly lucrative industrial secrets. But this—this just didn't make sense.

She quickly readjusted the dials and began to work her way through the microscopic coils of recombinant proteins, unable to shake the horrifying thought that the tissue she was looking at came from the brain of a person who had died from a disease created in her lab. *By her.*

How could it have been introduced into a human population without her knowledge? Had someone stolen her work? She felt nauseous.

The possibility of a Nexus experiment falling into the wrong hands had always been her greatest fear. It was an inherent risk with the kind of preemptive research they did here. And it was one of reasons for the all the secrecy and security.

She tweaked the dial, leaned closer to the screen, perspiration beading on her forehead. For years she'd been working on isolating the agent that caused an aggressive form of transmissible spongiform encephalopathy—or TSE—in the Blacklands bonobo troop. The disease was related to mad cow disease or Creutzfeldt-Jakob disease in humans. But while those illnesses took years to manifest, this particular TSE ate through the brains of bonobos like wildfire and caused intense aggression in the host, which in turn helped facilitate the spread of the pathogen through bodily fluids. Death came in a matter of days.

It was frightening to witness.

Her father and mother had been the first to identify the rare disease, and Paige, picking up on the work of her parents, had finally isolated the causative agent more than a decade later.

The result was earth-shattering. Her findings went against the grain of all current scientific thinking, yet she'd been unable to share her discovery with the rest of the world because of her legal obligations to Nexus.

Once she'd isolated the causative agent, she'd experimented by manipulating DNA and found that she could create a whole subset of TSE-style pathogens that affected the primate brain in different ways. Then, using her parents' observations, she was able to zero in on an antidote that was currently in the testing phase.

The pathogen she was looking at right now was unmistakably one of her recombinant diseases, a virulent variation of the original bonobo pathogen that, if released, had the potential to spread like wildfire in the human population.

Paige sat back. She felt shaky. Hot. She tried to breathe slowly, tried to tell herself there *had* to be a logical explanation for this. But who could she ask? She'd be fired, possibly even prosecuted, just for taking the sample. A confidentiality breach at Nexus was a deadly serious offense.

Then she sensed it again—a sudden movement behind the glass. Paige jumped, spun round and bumped her knee against the station. But she couldn't see anyone. She cursed softly. She was imagining things.

She'd lost her sense of control, and this was dangerous.

It was time to get out of the hot zone. Besides, she needed to digest what she'd just seen. She had to formulate the questions before she could even begin to hypothesize a scenario that might explain her horrific discovery.

Paige pushed her chair back and stood, feeling vaguely nauseous and way overheated in her suit. She lumbered over to the steel door, reached for the circular air lock, and hesitated. She shouldn't leave the tissue samples where someone might find them. Although this was her private lab and access was limited to her alone, after what she'd seen tonight, she wasn't taking chances.

She moved back to the lab table, collected the evidence, placed it in a waste carton, and waddled over to the small on-site incinerator. She dropped the carton into the hatch, sealed the door.

Paige watched the glow of flame through the little glass window, making doubly sure the evidence was completely devoured. This was one incineration she certainly wasn't going to log, and that, too, was breaking Nexus protocol.

By stealing that vial this morning, she'd opened some kind of Pandora's box.

She exited the lab with a lump of fear in her throat.

Rafiq quickly replaced the hard drive cover and consulted his handheld device. The light glowed red. He swore softly. It should be a steady green if the transmitter he'd just installed in the computer was emitting the correct signal for wireless uplink. He peeked up over the desk, keeping a check on the scientist working in the lab. He hadn't expected anyone to be in here at this hour.

He tensed as he saw the person in the blue hazmat suit heading toward the pressurized door. Whoever was in that suit could be through the decontamination showers and heading his way within a matter of minutes. He checked his watch. He had only one chance to make this work.

Rafiq quickly began to unscrew the hard drive cover again.

Paige pulled her *hijab* over her hair and fastened it at her neck. Even though the lab base was American she still wore a scarf and long skirt out of respect for the local Hamānians who worked on the compound.

She walked into her office and paused. It was as if the chemistry of the air had somehow shifted. She shook off the sensation, putting it down to guilt and the enormity of what she had just discovered in her lab.

She started down the dim corridor, a row of small orange night-lights glowing along the ceiling. Her long skirt swished about her ankles as she moved.

A raucous screech sliced the air. Paige gasped and jerked sideways. Then she laughed softly, nervously. It was just the chimps sensing her passing. She stepped up to the door on her right and peered through a small glass window above an orange-and-black biohazard sign.

The primates in cages looked surreal in the eerie glow of the night-lights. Regret rippled through her.

This was the part of her work that did not sit easy with her. She preferred seeing the chimps in the wild—like when she was a kid. She used to spend hours watching them in the jungle with her mom and dad at her side. She placed her palm against the glass, for a moment holding on to the sweet nostalgia, using it to ground herself. Then she noticed that the two big male chimps at the back of the room were leaping wildly up and down in their cages, baring incisors and pink gums in a threatening grimace. Paige frowned.

The males usually only acted that way in the presence of another strange male. Perhaps they were just picking up on her own edginess. She gathered the ends of her *hijab* tighter around her neck, suddenly needing to get back to her room, her photographs, her things.

She made for the exit at the end of the corridor.

But as she raised her identity card to swipe it through the slot, she realized she'd left her car keys in her office. It was a damn good thing she'd pulled herself out of the lab when she had. She clearly wasn't thinking straight. She walked briskly back to her office, heels clacking along the polished floor. She yanked open her desk drawer, reached for the keys…and a gloved hand clamped down hard over her wrist.

Shock slammed through her.

She opened her mouth to scream, but before any sound could escape her throat, another gloved hand smacked down hard over her lips. Her eyes watered with the pain.

Her attacker yanked her backward, hard up against his body, and he pressed the cold blade of a knife under her chin.

For a terrifying moment Paige couldn't breathe. Then her brain kicked back into gear. She concentrated on inhaling through her nose, willing herself to stay calm, to take in detail. He was big. Incredibly strong. Hard athletic body. There was a hint of clove and bergamot in the rough fabric of his clothes. She could also detect the scent of camels and saddle polish on his gloves. Her panic doubled.

How had he gotten past security?

He spun her round sharply, and Paige used the moment to lurch away from him, her movement so wild it sent her flying to the floor. She scrambled to her feet, slipping on the polished surface, tripping over her long skirt as she tried to get away.

He grabbed the back of her *hijab* in an effort to stop her, but she jerked against the resistance. The scarf pulled free from her neck and hair, and Paige began to race for the exit, holding the hem of her skirt high, praying the guards would see her on the surveillance system. If she could just get to the door, she could punch the alarm…

But he was on her, had her by the hair and the waist. Flight was no longer an option. She had to fight. She whirled round, tore at his turban, trying to expose his face to the cameras.

The black cloth came away from his face in her fist, and Paige gasped.

Her second of hesitation cost her, and he had his dagger back up against her throat and her arm wrenched so hard behind her back that tears leaked from her eyes.

She froze, not daring to move against the blade, her heart thudding hard.

His oil-black eyes pierced hers and they glittered with anger. He was breathing heavily.

Paige tried to swallow.

The man was fiercely beautiful, with dark olive skin, shoulder-length black hair, and a tattoo on his angular cheekbone. It was the tattoo that had made her gasp.

She stared at it now—the unmistakable Arabic lettering that symbolized the Silent Revolution, the underground movement that lay in wait, ready to overthrow the sultan of Hamān when the sign came.

The display of that symbol was punishable by instant death in this country. Sultan Sadiq bin Zafir bin Omar al-Qaadr had personally decreed that every citizen in the land had the right to mete out that death penalty in any way he chose if he so much as even glimpsed the symbol.

Her attacker was a walking affront to the ruler of Hamān.

But why was he here? What could a revolutionary possibly want with her?

Cautiously, Paige allowed her eyes to take in the rest of his powerful frame.

He was dressed completely in black. A burlap tunic covered loose cotton pants that were bound at his ankles with thongs. He had another knife strapped to his ankle. A band of old black leather crossed diagonally over his chest and a scimitar was sheathed at his waist. A coil of rope hung from his belt, as did a leather pouch.

A lump of fear and awe ballooned painfully in her throat. "What...what do you want with me?" she whispered hoarsely in Arabic.

Rafiq cursed bitterly as he realized who he held at knifepoint. *Dr. Paige Sterling.* And even more beautiful in the flesh. This was the last bloody thing he needed. His mission was clear—break into the lab, install the wireless transmitting device, set up a receiving station within radius of the device, uplink to satellite for remote access to the Nexus mainframe, and then get the hell out of Hamān the minute the download was complete.

Dr. Sterling was *not* part of the deal. She was off limits. *What the hell would he do now?*

He couldn't just leave her. Nor could he kill her. She was key to all this, and her dead body would most certainly alert the Cabal, the group of power-hungry men masterminding the threat against the U.S. So would kidnapping her. If Dr. Sterling—creator of their lethal bioweapon—suddenly went missing, millions in Chicago, Los Angeles and New York could be dead before the week was out.

He swore again. The clock was ticking. He had to move fast. He leaned close to the beautifully elegant face with perfect skin and cool pewter eyes—the face of evil genius he'd first glimpsed on the LCD screen back in the Force du Sable situation room on São Diogo Island. But somehow, in person, Paige Sterling didn't look so capable of pure evil. And right now, in his hands, she felt more than a little vulnerable.

Looks were deceiving, Rafiq told himself. And none more so than those of a highly intelligent, cunning and attractive woman. "How did you get to the lab tonight, Dr. Sterling?" he asked in English, his voice low.

Her eyes flared in surprise at the use of her name, and at his command of English. Then they narrowed, her lips flattening into a tight line. She glared at him, said nothing.

She *was* tough.

He tightened his grip on her arm, angled the hooked point of his *jambiya* blade up into her neck, just short of piercing her skin. "You *will* answer my questions, Doctor. Do you understand this?"

She nodded, ever so slightly, careful not to break her own skin against his dagger. Even so, the small movement forced the razor-sharp tip of his blade into her neck. She sucked in her breath sharply and her eyes widened in fear.

A small drop of dark-red blood began to bead through broken skin at the point of his knife. Rafiq watched it trickle down the pale column of her neck, a feeling of unease tightening through him. "Tell me how you got from the compound residence to the lab tonight." He released the pressure of the blade so that she could talk.

"Company SUV," her whisper was hoarse.

"It's…brown…parked in the lot outside. I…I came back for the keys."

Rafiq's eyes flashed back to the open drawer in her office. He edged her back down the corridor, toward the desk. "Take them. We'll use your ID to get out."

She reached for the drawer and removed the key chain. Rafiq noted her hand was steady in spite of the fear in her eyes. It shouldn't surprise him. She'd have to be mentally tough to work the way she did in max containment. She might be all pale light and elegant angles on the outside, but she had to have a heart of ice to do the kind of black biology they suspected her of. This woman killed innocent people.

Rafiq steeled his jaw, dug his fingers deeper into her arm just above the elbow, and steered her sharply down the corridor, using his remote to click in false video feeds as they passed under the cameras.

They exited through a side entrance on the ground floor, the dry desert air hitting them like a wall.

Her vehicle was the only one in the lot. It was parked at the far corner, up against the building. He led her along the wall, staying in the shadows. He opened the driver's side door. "Get in," he whispered.

She didn't move. Her eyes held his, defiant. With a jolt of irritation, he placed his hand on her head, forced her down into the driver's seat, and closed the door. He scanned the lot quickly. There was still no one in sight.

He crouched down, rolled under the SUV, and he used his *jambiya* to sabotage the brake line and hose. He waited until enough of the slippery fluid had dripped down on to the paving to insure the puddle would be noticeable.

He rolled out from under the vehicle, opened the passenger side door, slid into the seat. He handed her the keys as he pressed his dagger against her lower ribs. "Now drive. Nice and normal."

She glared at him.

"Do it."

Paige started the engine, perspiration beading over her lip, her heart racing. He maneuvered the bulk of his frame down below the dash and lowered his head to the seat, but he kept the point of his dagger pressed into her clothing. She could feel the tip of the blade poking through the fabric, and she could feel the dampness of blood under her collar—a reminder of just how sharp that dagger was.

She swallowed, engaged the gears and drove slowly, wheels crunching over sand that had blown across the paved lot during the day. Her mind scrambled wildly for a plan of escape.

She had to do something. If she went any farther with her assailant, she'd wind up dead. She was certain of it. She neared the guard hut, depressed the brakes. They felt soft. Her mouth went bone-dry. So *that's* what he'd been doing under the car. She wound down her window slowly as she approached the sentry hut.

Mahmoud Hassim was on duty tonight. He looked up from his book, smiled, his teeth white in the neon light of his cubicle. "Good evening, Dr. Sterling." He set his book down, reached out of his window for her pass.

She hesitated.

The dagger blade pressed harder into her ribs. One upward thrust would pierce her liver. Even if she gave Mahmoud a sign, even if he did manage to sound the alarm, she'd bleed to death before they could get her into the main hospital, miles away from the compound. Perspiration prickled her brow and slicked down between her breasts. She reached for her pass, handed it to Mahmoud.

His smiled faded slightly. "Are you okay, Doctor?"

She pressed her lips together, nodded.

Mahmoud studied her for a second too long.

"I...I'm fine. Mahmoud, thank you." She forced a smile. "I'm just tired."

He scanned her pass. "Much too late to be working, even for you, Dr. Sterling." He handed it back to her as the boom lifted. She drove slowly through.

Her assailant sat up in the passenger seat as soon as they disappeared from the sentry's sight.

"Go the coast road," he commanded.

Blood drained from her head. The coast road was a series of chilling hairpin bends along precipitous sandstone cliffs that plunged sheer into the depths of the Red Sea.

And he'd damaged her brakes.

If her car went over... "What...what do you want with me?"

"Just drive."

Paige clutched the wheel, her palms damp. She was as good as dead.

Chapter 2

The headlights of her SUV panned round, throwing a row of date palms into stark relief. Paige stiffened—after that row of trees came the first killer bend.

"Bring the vehicle to a stop," he said suddenly. "Don't use the brakes. Gear down. And stay on the road."

Her mind raced. What was he going to do? Get out and force her to drive over the cliff? How? *Why?* If he was a member of the underground, what could he possibly want with her? She ground the vehicle to a stop against the gears and engaged the hand brake. She tested the brake pedal. It flopped flat to the floor. Dread pooled in her stomach.

He threw open the passenger door, got out, marched round to the driver's side, yanked her door open. "Out."

Relief punched through her. He wasn't going to send her over with the car. She lifted her skirt and climbed down onto the road, desperate for another vehicle to come by, knowing it was close to an impossibility at this hour. If any of her colleagues were even awake, they'd be at the clubhouse, shooting pool, drinking smuggled liquor and chewing mildly narcotic qat—hardly in any shape to rescue her. She spent so little time with them anyway, they probably wouldn't even notice her missing for days.

"Turn around."

She obeyed. He wrenched her wrists sharply behind her back, bound them with rope. Then he crouched down and lifted her skirt. Panic wedged into her chest. For the first time, she felt conscious of her femininity, and vulnerable because of it. She was utterly defenseless against this powerful male.

It took a second before she realized what he was doing. He was tying the one end of the rope he'd bound around her wrists to her ankle, effectively hobbling her like a camel.

Damn the bastard.

If he was trying to subjugate her mentally as well as physically, he'd just succeeded. And if she tried to run now, she'd be flat on her face in the sand in a heartbeat. *Sand.* She could leave footprints in the sand!

Paige began to edge off the asphalt. But he saw what she was doing instantly. He grabbed her, jerked her sharply back onto the road, and brought his mouth so close to hers she could feel the warmth of his breath against her lips.

"Do not make this any more difficult on yourself, Dr. Sterling." His *r*'s growled low in his throat sending a hot-cold shiver down her spine. "Stay on the pavement. Do *only* what I say, *when* I say it, understand?" His obsidian eyes bored into hers, catching the gleam of the headlights. "Do not underestimate me, Doctor. Because once your vehicle goes over that cliff—" he pointed to the black void over the Red Sea "—no one is going to come looking for you. And I mean *no one*. Do you understand what that means?"

Oh, God, she understood all right. If everyone thought she was dead, she may as well be.

"Now wait here."

He climbed into the driver's seat, started the engine, put the car into gear.

Paige instantly shuffled backward onto the sand again, quickly making as many telltale scuff marks as she could. But she stilled as she saw her car heading straight for the cliff, the driver's side door hanging open.

The SUV gathered speed, hit the first S in the bend, bounced from tar onto sand, and careened toward the cliff.

Her breath lodged in her throat.

But just before her car smashed into the small white marker rocks along the cliff edge, he dived from the door and rolled clear of the vehicle.

Paige watched in numb horror as the SUV lurched sideways, teetered on the rocks for a nanosecond, then plunged headfirst into the black void.

There was a moment of deathly silence…then metal hit rock with a stomach-churning crunch. Then another, and another, as her car bounced and bashed and splintered its way down to the Red Sea.

He turned and raced back toward her.

There was one more metallic crunch followed by an explosive boom that rocked the ground under her feet. A ball of fire whooshed into the moonless sky turning him into a black silhouette as he sprinted toward her. Behind him more fireballs burst and crackled into the night.

Paige couldn't move.

All she could do was stare and recall that she'd just had the gas tank filled, along with the two spare cans in the back.

He grabbed her arm, spun her round, crouched down and slashed the rope that bound her ankles and wrists. Then he saw the scuff marks in the sand. He cursed, brushed them over with quick flicks of his hand, holding her wrist in vise-like grip with the other. She winced at the pressure. She'd angered him, pushed him too far. Talons of fear raked at her heart. What was he going to do with her now?

She glanced wildly around. There was nothing for miles but black desert and moonless sky.

He jerked her toward him. "Now, run, Doctor, like your life depends on it," he growled. *"Because it does."*

He turned and yanked her after him. Paige lurched forward, tripping over the hem of her skirt. She managed to right herself, grasp the fabric of her skirt in her free hand and hoist it up above her knees as she flailed wildly in his wake.

She could barely keep up. He was sprinting, sticking to the hard surface of the road where they would leave no prints. It took every ounce of her concentration to just stay upright. She began to pant. Hot dry air rasped against her throat, stung her chest. She couldn't go on much longer.

She could hear the wail of sirens now, rising in the distance, the sounds closing in on them from two opposite directions—the residential complex to the south, and the lab buildings to the north. There was always a Nexus emergency crew on standby at the lab in the event of a chemical fire. They must have heard the explosion, seen the ball of orange in the sky. The whine of an ambulance joined the sound of fire engines as emergency personnel raced to the scene of the fireball…and she raced away from it.

Panic clutched her heart.

Each step was taking her farther from rescue. The emergency crews would reach the scene, see her vehicle tracks and immediately assume she'd gone over the cliff. They'd write her off as dead. She could almost see them, dark silhouettes huddled together, looking over the edge, talking in low voices. They'd retrace her steps. Mahmoud would tell them she'd been working late, that she'd looked tired, unwell. They'd find a puddle of brake fluid in the parking lot, assume her brakes had failed along that first hairpin bend. And even if they sent divers to look for her body and came up empty-handed, they'd assume the notorious hammerhead sharks and currents had taken what was left of her.

Paige felt sick at the thought.

The sirens grew louder, filling the desert night. They'd be coming along this stretch of road any minute. Perhaps they'd see her. For a moment, hope flared.

But her kidnapper killed it. He yanked her off the road and onto hard, rocky ground that seemed to suck up what little starlight they had used to find their way. Mica glinted evilly in the sharp edges of flint, and Paige had to redouble her efforts to remain upright on the uneven terrain. This man knew what he was doing. They'd leave no obvious tracks on this rocky expanse. And no one would even think to come looking with dogs because she was supposed to be dead.

The implications suddenly hit her full force.

She could *not* let this man take her from the U.S. compound into one of the oldest countries in Arabia—a mysterious land completely cut off from the West where no travelers or journalists were ever permitted to set foot.

A land ruled by a despotic sultan who'd declared it law that a woman travel only in the company of a male with authorized travel papers, and that she be fully covered by the traditional black *chador.*

She *had* to try to escape, stay on familiar ground. This was her last and only chance, because once he took her into that desert, she'd be at his mercy, and at the mercy of the sultan's notorious Land Command, should they find her.

The sand underfoot grew thick and soft as they neared the perimeter fence. Paige stumbled, fell, her knee slamming into the razor-sharp edge of a flint rock. She gasped and doubled over as pain sparked through her kneecap.

He jerked to a stop, wordlessly scooped her to her feet and slid his arm firmly around her waist. "Keep going," he said as he moved forward, lifting her so that she could keep weight off her injured knee.

Blood trickled down the inside of her calf as Paige half limped, half ran, her body snug against his solid frame.

They reached the 10-foot-high electrified fence trimmed with razor wire, and he stopped. Thankful, she dug her hands into her waist, bent over, trying to catch her breath. She was panting hard, her lungs raw. She looked slowly up at the fence. *What now?*

"Go under." He jerked his chin toward the base of the wire. She followed the movement, saw the hole in the sand. Her eyes shot back to his. He couldn't possibly expect her to crawl through that? It was too shallow. She'd connect with the wire. She knew just what kind of voltage pulsed through this thing. It would fry her.

"Now! On your stomach." He shoved her to the ground, forced her flat onto the damp soil. "Stay low." He growled, increasing pressure against the small of her back so that her belly pressed down hard into the sand. She didn't dare fight back for fear of connecting with the fence.

Paige took a deep, shaky breath, closed her eyes, and began to squirm carefully through the sand. Her long skirt had other ideas. It tangled around her legs, making forward movement close to impossible. She paused for a moment, trying to think this through. She managed to work a system of wiggling her hips sideways, then forward, using her pelvis, inching her body through the sand until she could claw her way out the other side.

She got to her knees, pushed her hair out of her face and the sheer black vastness of the desert ahead hit her. Terror clawed through her heart. She had to do something. Now. Before they left the safety of the compound. She saw the rock at her side. She could bash him on the head while he was crawling under the fence, exposed, vulnerable. If she was lucky, he'd jerk up and electrocute himself and the alarms would go off. Help would come.

She edged her hand out sideways and slowly fingered the sand. She found the rock, closed her fist over it. She sucked in her breath sharply, flung her arm high into the air, and spun round, bringing the rock down with all her might.

It slammed dully into sand as he rolled to the side. He was on his feet before she could even blink. He hauled her up, twisting her arm sharply.

"You want to play hardball, Doctor?" His voice was rough in his throat. Her eyes watered in pain and frustration.

"Well, you've made your choice." He forced her wrists together and bound them so tightly she feared he was cutting off blood supply. He gave a low whistle, and a hobbled camel materialized from the blackness. Almost instantly Paige could detect the scent of the worn leather saddle, the faint aroma of spice and incense that permeated the woven saddle cloths—the same scents she'd identified on his clothing in the lab. She had an acute sense of smell. Fear only sharpened it.

He untied the camel's legs, and couched the beast with a sharp cluck of his tongue.

"Get on."

Paige hesitated. She could ride horses, but she'd never mounted a camel.

"Just climb into the saddle."

She shot a last and desperate look at the perimeter fence and saw his hand going for his *jambiya* as she did. She gritted her teeth and climbed awkwardly into the saddle, her long skirt riding up her thighs, her bound wrists making her clumsy. The camel sensed her inexperience and fear instantly. He grunted and began to spit in protest. But her assailant took firm hold of the rope attached to the animal's nose ring, and he whispered in soft Arabic, gently stroking the beast's neck, calming him.

His sudden tenderness took Paige by surprise.

The way he was handling this beast showed he had capacity for compassion, and that gave her a small spark of hope.

Maybe if she played her cards right, just maybe if she stopped fighting him, she'd be okay…at least until she figured out what in hell he wanted with her.

Once he had the camel settled, he strapped her hands to the saddle horn and he left her sitting there, straddled over the animal, while he worked quickly to refill the hole they'd just crawled through. Paige watched him smooth sand over it using a soft brush from his camel bag. She noted that in spite of his haste, his movements were economical, calm and methodical. He was in complete control. She related to that, and in some strange way his control calmed her a little.

He secured his shovel to the camel bag, climbed up into the saddle and wedged himself in behind her in a disturbingly intimate fashion—his iron-hard thighs bracketing her bare legs, his groin pushing hard into her butt. Paige swallowed sharply.

This was clearly a saddle made for one.

His reached around her, his arms and scent enveloping her as he picked up the reins. She could feel the hilt of his *jambiya* against her hip and the steady beat of his heart against her back. He nudged the camel's neck with his heels, the motion squeezing his thighs tighter around her. An unwelcome frisson of sexual energy shot through her body from head to toe. Paige blinked.

This was absurd. The man was kidnapping her. How could she possibly feel turned on by his touch? It had to be a chemical reaction to the intimate seating arrangements, pure and simple. Didn't mean she had to like it.

But every nerve in her body was suddenly acutely aware of him. It had to be the fear, she told herself in panic. The adrenaline. But she could no more bury her own sudden physical awareness than she could the raw fear of facing this vast desert with this fearsomely attractive—and dangerous—underground rebel.

He nudged the camel again and it rose like a wobbly leviathan. He flicked the reins and the animal rocked forward, lolling from side to side like a giraffe as it moved. Paige hung on, trying to adapt to the awkward rolling motion. No wonder they called these animals ships of the desert—she'd be seasick in minutes at this rate. Thinking of her stomach made her realize she hadn't eaten since morning—yesterday morning. She wondered if she'd ever see the inside of the Nexus cafeteria again, if she'd ever see Western civilization again.

He flicked the reins, urging their mount straight into a gallop. Paige inhaled sharply as she lurched sideways in the seat, her skirt riding higher up her thighs. But he clenched her even tighter between his legs, holding her steady with his body, giving her his rhythm. She realized that fighting the movement only made things worse. She forced herself to clear her mind and to relax into the motion, into him, flowing with his rhythmic pace, the movement of his warm body against hers, the tempo of the camels hooves over the sand...until all three of them operated as one smooth unit, racing across the vast expanse of sand and darkness.

Their speed made the hot desert air move like velvet over her skin. Paige closed her eyes, enjoying the sensation, and for a wild fleeting instant her heart soared, free. But she sobered instantly, almost losing the rhythm again as she did. She'd just been kidnapped. And she had no idea why.

Rafiq kept a steady pace over the next twenty miles, using the stars as his guide. He'd forgotten just how damn good it felt to ride the desert at night. And he was certainly not complaining about how good it felt to have a beautiful woman between his thighs.

He loved women, everything about them—as long as he was always in control, as long as he never engaged his heart. That had happened only once.

It would never happen again.

But this—this was just pure sensual pleasure. He allowed himself to lean forward to feel her soft hair against his cheek, to drink in her fragrance. It was soapy, clean, underlaid with the faint hint of chemicals from the decontamination showers. But in her clothes he could detect lingering perfume—something lemony with a touch of gardenia and frankincense. It surprised him slightly, that this cool and calculating scientist was not above feminine wiles. And the fact that she'd chosen a local Arabian scent was even more intriguing. Curiosity rustled through him.

The doctor was all his for the next few days. Her secrets were his to discover.

He slowed the camel as they neared the paved road that would lead them to Na'jif. He needed to give the animal a break. It would be at least another hour before they arrived at the gates of the ancient walled city where he'd rented a suite of rooms and stashed his gear for the uplink.

But the instant he slowed, Paige struggled to turn around in the seat but couldn't, not with her hands tied to the saddle horn. "Where are you taking me?" she demanded.

He raised his brow. That was not fear in her voice, it was determination laced with frustration. This was a woman accustomed to getting her own way, just as he was a man accustomed to getting his.

"To Na'jif," he said

"Why?" she snapped. "Who *are* you? What do you want from me? Industrial secrets? Is that what this about? You want ransom money from Nexus?"

A soft snort escaped him. "Ransom money?" He leaned forward, placed his mouth against her ear where he could feel the soft fuzz of her lobe against his bottom lip. "You honestly think I want money, Doctor?" he whispered against her ear, feeling a shudder chase through her body as he did.

"What…is it that you want, then?" She sounded nervous now.

"I want the antidote, Paige," he whispered into her ear, deliberately using her first name for the first time, pushing familiarity as a power ploy. "I came for the antidote."

Her body tensed instantly. "What antidote?" she asked quietly.

"The antidote to the bioweapon you created."

"*Bioweapon?* Are you crazy?" She struggled desperately to turn around again, but he held her firmly in place with his thighs.

"Do not play games with me, Dr. Sterling," he growled. "You know *exactly* what I'm talking about."

She strained against her bonds. "No, I do not! Why don't you tell me? Can…can you just untie me so that I can talk to you properly?"

He ignored her request. "I want the vaccine for the disease you engineered in your lab, the one that eats into human brains, makes people violent, makes them kill, leaves them dead within days."

She went dead silent. She stopped struggling and stared out over the dark desert. "I engineered no such agent," she said finally, her voice quiet and level.

Irritation flared in him. "This game will only get you hurt, Doctor. We know what you did. We know that what you made is neither virus, nor bacteria. It's a recombinant form of a rare TSE found only in pygmy chimps from the Blacklands region of the Congo. And you genetically manipulated it. You took your parents' discovery and used it to create a whole new subset of lethal TSEs. Isn't that right, Doctor?"

This was what their intel had pointed to, the reason he'd

been dispatched to the Nexus lab. But his orders had been simply to get data from the computers, not take the doctor herself. But now that he had her, he was going to pump her for as much information as he could.

She didn't say a word. She sat there, her body strangely limp, rocked only by the motion of the camel. The minutes stretched. Finally she spoke. "I…I have no idea what you're talking about," she said very softly. Too softly. He could hear raw fear in her tone now.

He gave a forced laugh. "You created a monster, Paige. And you are going to help us stop it."

Panic licked through her. What did he mean? Did he *know* her pathogen had appeared in a human population in the Congo? And how did this Hamānian rebel know this? The country was almost entirely cut off from the rest of the world. Even phones were outlawed.

Paige felt dizzy. Somehow this man knew *exactly* what she'd been working on all her life. He knew about her parents. He knew what she'd believed to be top secret…and more. He appeared to know something about what was happening in Quadrant 3, because tonight was the first time in *her* life she'd seen her recombinant pathogen in the brains of humans. To her knowledge, her work had *never* been tested on humans, and neither had her vaccine—only in primates. It was theory, meant for extrapolation. For research. That was the Nexus Research and Development Corporation's mandate—create the diseases, find the cures, then patent them and store them until the time arose to profit from them through their U.S. division, BioMed Pharmaceutical. It was a high-tech game of medical futures and it was a mercenary approach that didn't always sit easily on Paige's shoulders, but she reasoned that, given the new world order, it was highly unlikely that the next emerging virus was going to come from a jungle.

It was going to come from a man-made bioreactor, and it could well be an enemy that created it.

To think that this kind of science was not being bent toward weapons and crime, would be to ignore the reality of human nature in the modern world. The Nexus goal was to be prepared for that eventuality, to have the cutting-edge scientific tools and weapons—in this case, anti-dotes—to combat any new biological threat developed by the wrong hands. And to sell those antidotes—at a high price, of course—to a populace or government that would be more than desperate to pay for them. But that was just the way of the corporate world and the pharmaceutical industry. Without the private sector, the kind of ground-breaking work she was doing wouldn't be possible. She'd never have had the funding.

But this…this made her feel sick. Her work was supposed to be for the greater good. Not evil.

"Do you need to hear more, Dr. Sterling?" His voice had taken on a rough and patronizing tone. "Or has your memory been sufficiently jogged?"

She said nothing. She didn't know how this man knew what she was doing, who he was working for, or why she'd been kidnapped. She only knew that he was dangerous, and she didn't want to give him any more information. Right now silence was her best defense, at least until she could figure out who he worked for, and why he really wanted her.

But suddenly his body went rigid against hers. Paige glanced up, and she saw what he'd seen. Headlights. From three jeeps on the road up ahead. Soldiers stood around them.

The Royal Land Command.

Her heart began to race. She wasn't wearing the legislated *chador!* Her legs were exposed.

Both were crimes punishable by death in Hamān.

And her hands were bound—she couldn't even begin to pull her skirt down over her naked legs. Panic clawed through her. Paige wriggled frantically in the saddle, trying to get her skirt to move down her thighs and cover her nakedness. But it was impossible. And even if she did manage to cover herself, it would be of no use. The man she was traveling with bore the mark of the Silent Revolution. They would slit his throat on the spot. And hers, too.

A spotlight swept over the desert catching them briefly. It panned back, settling on them. Paige began to shake. She closed her eyes, and said a silent prayer.

Chapter 3

05:00 Charlie, Hamānian desert, Thursday, October 2

Her assailant reached around her with his *jambiya,* and slashed the rope that bound her wrists to the saddle horn. "Quick, throw your leg over the horn," he hissed as he flipped his turban over his face. "Sit sidesaddle so you can pull your skirt down." He held her by the waist as she swung her leg over the horn, and wriggled her skirt down.

He pulled her scarf up over her hair. "Wrap the end over your face," he whispered hotly. "You are my wife, understand? Keep your eyes averted at all times. Look only at the ground, never at anyone's face. Do *not* open your mouth."

She did as he said. She knew it was in her own best interests, but his commands were the kind of thing women in Hamān had to endure on a daily basis, thanks to the sick whims of Sultan Sadiq bin Zafir bin Omar al-Qaadr—or the Scarred Sultan, as they called him.

Everyone in Hamān knew the sultan's laws had less to do with upholding ancient tradition and culture than they had to do with oppressing his people, instilling a culture of fear and insuring his tyrannical hold on power. The soldiers of the Royal Land Command were his henchmen, his personal police force. They had unprecedented powers and a dark reputation for abusing them.

Her wrists throbbed badly where rope had cut into her skin. But she couldn't think about that. She clutched her scarf tightly over her face as they neared the jeeps. Turning away was not an option now. It would guarantee chase— even she could see that.

Paige could hear snatches of conversation as they drew closer, and she could feel the slow, steady thud of her captor's heart against her back. This man was not afraid, yet his limbs were hard with tension, braced for a fight. And she was between a rock and one very tough place—because right now her kidnapper was the lesser of two evils.

The soldiers adjusted their weapons as they neared. One stepped forward. "Halt!"

He reined in the camel.

The soldier approached them. The desert had gone so quiet she could hear his boots squeak in the sand. He shone a flashlight up into their faces. She blinked, kept her eyes cast down.

"Papers!" he demanded in Arabic.

Oh God, please, please let him have papers.

She felt her captor move behind her. She stared at the soldier's boots, praying he wouldn't kill her on the spot for not wearing the regulation garment.

Paige heard the rustle of papers being handed down, saw the soldier's hand take them. She hoped they were in order.

She heard the policeman flipping through the documents, and she tried to force herself to breathe. The irony wasn't lost on her. She didn't dare tell these men she'd been kidnapped at knifepoint. As a woman, they would consider it *her* fault, U.S. citizen or not. Such was the law in this country. There wasn't even a U.S. embassy she could turn to for help. The closest was in Saudi Arabia, over the border and oceans of sand.

The policeman stopped flipping. Paige slanted her eyes cautiously toward his hands. He was studying a photograph. "Quasim Rashid." He shone his flashlight into her captor's eyes. "You are Bedouin?"

"Yes."

"What are doing here, off the road?"

"My wife and I, we are going to Na'jif, sir." There was no hint of subservience in his voice. He probably couldn't be submissive if he tried.

The policeman picked up on it, too. It provoked him. He stepped closer to the camel.

Paige heard the click of a safety as one of the soldiers on the road trained his rifle on them. Her heart began to palpitate. The camel shuffled.

The policeman lowered his voice. "I repeat, what are you doing off the road at this time of night?"

"We were visiting our relatives. They have taken their animals out to graze in the Jiza'an valley, on the stubble of the wheat harvest. We are heading home now." He covered Paige more assertively with his body as he spoke. She leaned into him, taking refuge in his confidence.

"We are late because my wife took ill, sir. We had to rest

during the heat of the day." He hesitated, carefully timing his beats for effect. "She is with child, sir."

The man shone the flashlight into her face.

Breathe, Paige. Breathe.

"In the name of the Sultan, why is she not properly veiled?" he demanded.

"She will be, sir. As I said, she took ill, and her *chador,* it is unfortunately badly soiled. We have the correct clothing at home. Please, in the name of the Sultan, forgive us this transgression. It is another reason we travel in the dark, out of sight from those who may take offense."

The soldier walked slowly around the camel checking their gear, probably seeing what he could steal if he arrested them. A radio crackled up in one of the jeeps. The soldier paused. One of the soldiers turned the volume up. Paige could make out a few of the words—something about a vehicle explosion at the Nexus compound, a woman scientist dying.

Nexus officials must have informed the Command. The sultan kept meticulous track of the names and numbers of employees at the American base, and he only tolerated the corporation's presence in his country because of the massive financial donations paid annually into his coffers. He'd also made it absolutely clear that all Nexus employees would be subject to all Hamānian laws off the base. Her heart jackhammered and she clutched her scarf tighter over her face. Would they look at her more closely now?

The radio crackled again, and the men at the jeeps started to talk excitedly. This was probably the best action they'd seen all week.

The soldier handed the papers back and slapped the camel's rump hard. "Go!" The beast lurched sideways and serpentined its neck around in an effort to bite the soldier.

Her assailant held it expertly. Paige had no doubt that if he allowed his camel to injure a member of the Land Command, they'd be dead in an instant.

Her captor clucked his tongue, nudged the camel gently, calmly, with his heels, and they moved away into the dark as the men scrambled into the jeeps and fired the engines.

Paige exhaled sharply and slumped back against her captor's chest, unable to hold herself erect anymore. Her heart was still racing. The sound of blood rushing filled her ears. She tried to calm herself, drawing comfort from the smooth, solid movement of his body against hers. And again the irony hit her.

He'd untied her hands, but it made no difference. She was bound to him. She was his prisoner in this land, unable to move without him and his travel papers.

And he knew it.

The sound of the jeep engines gradually faded miles into the distance and the vast desert hush enveloped them. It was just the two of them now, an unlikely couple, alone in the night, strangely bonded by the certain death they'd just managed to escape.

They continued to travel in uneasy silence, along the straight desert road toward the ancient walled city of Na'jif. Paige could see it in the distance now—a great dark mass of shadow looming up out of the flat sands. And behind it, the violet light of dawn was beginning to seep into the sky as the sun rose somewhere behind the jagged peaks of the Asir Mountains.

Paige knew that behind that range lay the Rub Al-Khali, the vast Saudi Arabian desert. It was a place no one would find her—even if she did manage to make it over the mountains and across the border. Even if anyone did come looking for her.

Her only hope of survival right now was to stick with this man. And the more she could find out about him, the better.

Know thy enemy, Paige. Just like you have to understand your pathogens in order to control them, manipulate them, outsmart them.

"Is...is that really your name?" she asked softly. "Quasim Rashid? Are you Bedouin?"

"You *understood* what we were saying?" She heard the surprise in his tone.

"Yes, I speak Arabic."

He remained silent for a while. Something about his demeanor had changed after the interaction with the Land Command. It wasn't that he seemed less arrogant. But he did seem pensive, a little quieter in his movements. Almost brooding. She knew it had to kill him—a soldier of the Silent Revolution—submitting to the sultan's men like that. A part of her actually admired him for the way he'd handled it. Another part was simply thankful he'd gotten her through the roadblock alive. But that didn't change the fact she was still his captive.

"No," he said finally. "My name is not Quasim. It's Rafiq Zayed. I'm a professional soldier with the Force du Sable. It's a private military company based on São Diogo Island, off the coast of Angola."

Her brows shot up. "You're a *mercenary?*"

He said nothing.

"What...what do you want with *me?* Who has hired you?"

"I told you what I want, Paige."

She swallowed. She needed to look into his eyes, see if he was telling the truth, but this intimate saddle arrange-

ment made that impossible. She stared instead at the
looming silhouette of the walled city slowly taking shape
in the distance as dawn lightened the sky.

So he had a name. But was it real?

This man spoke the Hamānian dialect perfectly, and his
accent held all the complex nuances of the local tongue. It
was not an easy lingo to come by—the country had been
closed to outsiders for decades.

It was also virtually impossible to enter the country and
move around without authorized papers. Foreigners were
not welcome. Tourists were banned. And Hamānian travel
papers would not be easy to forge unless you had access
to the documents.

This man carried travel papers that passed inspection. He
knew where he was going, even in the night. He knew camels,
and he knew just how to speak to the Land Command.

And then there was the tattoo on his cheek.

Rafiq Zayed was a local, she was sure of it. And if he
was a member of the Hamānian underground, it meant his
fight, too, was local. If he wanted her work, it *had* to be
for the revolution.

She could sympathize with that. Anyone who had the
courage to try and overthrow the Scarred Sultan was okay
in her book.

But her work had not been designed as a weapon, no
matter the cause. In the wrong hands, her pathogens could
launch a global pandemic. She was already gravely concerned by what she'd discovered in that vial.

Besides, how did he know what she was working on?
Was there a spy within Nexus? And what did all of this
have to do with a private military company off the coast of
Angola, if in fact, that was the truth.

She had to keep him talking. She had to learn more. She needed to figure out what exactly he wanted of her. Then maybe she could negotiate.

"Force du Sable—that's a French name. Is it a French company that you work for?"

He said nothing, just swayed gently with the camel, his body, his groin, rocking against her in an undeniably sensual rhythm. She tried to push it from her mind and cleared her throat. "São Diogo Island was…it was not originally a French colony, was it?" She tried to speak normally but her voice felt thick. He *had* to know that she was feeling his arousal. He was probably enjoying it, damn him. "It's…Portuguese, isn't it?" She tried to clear her throat again. "Like Angola?"

"You know your geography. I'm impressed." His voice was laden with sensual undertones and guttural *r*'s that rolled beautifully somewhere low down in his throat. It was the kind of throaty accent that made something hot slide down her spine.

Paige closed her eyes, trying to get a grip on herself. "You don't sound French or Portuguese," she said more firmly. "You sound Hamānian. You look Hamānian. You *are* Hamānian, aren't you?"

His body tensed sharply, his thighs tightening along her legs. A shock of sexual awareness speared through her body. Paige caught her breath in surprise.

But he remained silent. He wasn't going to take the bait.

She took a very deep breath, steadied herself. "So…what's with the French, then? How come the French name for a mercenary organization based in Portuguese Africa?"

"Are you always so persistent with the questions, Doctor?"

"Maybe I'd just like to know who kidnapped me and why," she snapped in exasperation.

"I have nothing to hide, Paige," he said slowly in that throaty accent. "I used to be with the French Foreign Legion. I served my five-year contract with the organization, and I made some very close friends there—people I will die for to this day. We got together after we left, and we formed the FDS. That was 10 years ago." He paused. "And you already know what I want from you, Paige."

She could *feel* what he wanted, at least one level. The evidence was pressing firmly into her body this very minute.

"No, dammit, I don't!" She tried to squirm forward in the saddle, frustration and her own reaction to his proximity getting the better of her. "I have no idea what you are talking about. I know *nothing* about a bioweapon!"

There was another long stretch of silence. Oppressive. He was goading her, she was sure. She breathed slowly, straining to recapture her customary calm. If she could do it in the hot zone of her lab, then she could do it in the desert, she told herself. She would never match this guy in strength. Her best weapons were going to be her brain and her ability to stay cool. Lose those, and she had nothing.

"Okay," she said calmly. "Can you at least tell me who hired you?"

"The president of the United States."

Her brain reeled. The sun exploded over the ridge of purple mountains and rippled over the sand toward them, the yellow light instantly hot against her face.

She laughed nervously. "Yeah, right."

But he said nothing.

Was he serious?

Paige's stomach felt suddenly hollow. "That's…that's not possible."

Still he said nothing.

"I…I don't believe you."

"I don't care what you believe, Dr. Sterling. I just care to get my job done."

President John Elliot? She gripped the saddle horn with both hands, feeling suddenly unsteady. How *could* it be possible?

How could the president of the United States know what she was working on? And even if he did, even if he thought she'd manufactured a bioweapon and antidote, why on earth would he hire foreign mercenaries to come and get her?

The president didn't hire mercs. He used the CIA, covert agents—*not* a private security company. This man was lying. He *had* to be. He was a local rebel. He probably had nothing to do with the United States. He was trying to con her for some reason.

Then she thought again of the vial she'd taken from Quadrant 3, of the infected human brain she'd seen under her microscope. The word *bioweapon* hung like a sword over her consciousness. And dread began to circle her heart.

What if her pathogen really had somehow been turned into a weapon and tested in the Congo? Horror rose through her chest, closed around her windpipe.

Paige tried to swallow against it. "So…why…why would the president hire a private military company? What was wrong with all the other mechanisms available to him?"

"He's being held hostage, Paige."

"*The president?* By who?"

"I think you know this already."

She closed her eyes, trying to staunch the nausea riding up through her chest. "I told you, Rafiq, I don't know *anything.* I do medical research and development for Nexus. I do *not* create weapons. I have no idea what you're talking about."

He exhaled slowly behind her. She could feel his breath warm against her neck. She kept her eyes closed.

"President Elliot is being held hostage in the White House by a group that calls itself simply the Cabal. Over the last thirty years this organization has managed to infiltrate the most influential levels of the United States government, the private sector, and the military—even the Secret Service. The very system designed to protect the president is now holding him captive. If he so much as even thinks of turning to one of the traditional agencies available to him for help, your pathogen will be released instantly over New York, Los Angeles and Chicago."

Paige opened her eyes and blinked into hot light that now bounced sharply off miles of sand. "Why?" Her voice came out hoarse. "Why is he being held hostage?"

"The Cabal wants the president to step down by midnight October 13—eleven days from now—and hand his leadership over to Vice President Grayson Forbes. If he doesn't—"

"They will release my pathogen?"

"Correct."

"What about the vice president, what does he have to do with this?"

"Forbes is a member of the Cabal. If Elliot hands the presidency to him, they will have successfully staged a coup of one of the most powerful countries in the world." He paused. "The FDS cannot let that happen. We have been hired to stop them. And to do it, we need to know more about your pathogen. And we *need* that antidote."

Oh, God, this was a bad dream. It had to be. She'd wake up. "Who…who is behind this Cabal?"

"I was kind of hoping you'd tell me, Doctor."

She swung round in the tight saddle, almost dislodging herself, but she managed to keep her body twisted around to face his, her breasts brushing uncomfortably against his chest. "You have *got* to believe me. I have nothing to do with this!"

His black eyes narrowed and bored down into hers. A small muscle pulsed under his tattoo. His mouth—wide, sculpted—was so close to hers. He leaned forward, his lips almost touching hers. "You have *everything* to do with this, Doctor," he whispered. "*You* created this bioweapon. *You* work for a Cabal-controlled corporation—"

"I know nothing about this Cabal! I work for Nexus—"

"Like I said, a *Cabal-controlled* corporation."

"Nexus?"

His eyes watched hers, dark, intent, intimidating.

"I…I do research and development for the creation of medicines…" Her voice trailed off as she thought of Q3, of what she'd seen under her microscope. Perspiration pricked her skin. "I…I never weaponized anything."

He snorted harshly. "What exactly did you think you were doing in a secret offshore lab in a country like Hamān? Making *medicine?* That's a laugh."

Panic nipped at her. "Damn you! Stop! Stop this camel. Listen to me."

His eyes glinted mischievously, and he nudged the camel forward even faster, almost throwing her.

Damn this man to hell!

She flung her hand back, gripped the horn behind her, trying to steady herself, but she kept her body twisted awkwardly to face his, her breasts bumping against his chest as they moved. She *had* to see his eyes. "*If* what you are saying is true, *if* my pathogen is being used in this way, someone *else* has weaponized it. Don't you see? I've been *used,* dammit! My work has been stolen." She was shaking now. All she could think of was how her prion pathogens affected bonobos—how the primates went demented within hours, started attacking each other…biting, ripping even their own skin, killing their mates, injuring their young. By affecting the brain, the disease drove its hosts to spread the pathogen through blood and saliva and open wounds…before the hosts died a horrible, messy death within mere days. If this turned up in humans…in places as densely populated as Los Angeles, New York, Chicago…

Oh God, what had she done?

"We…we cannot let this happen!"

His thick black brows hooked up in surprise, and he slowed his animal instantly. *"We?"*

"That's right, *we* have to stop this, Rafiq. That pathogen will spread like wildfire through those cities. This is the worst kind of terror—"

"Which is why we need that antidote, Doctor."

Paige searched his liquid black eyes, looking for a sign of emotion, some hint that would tell her he was lying. But his expression remained unchanged, his eyes steady. Her heart sank.

She shifted slowly around in the saddle, and she stared over the camel's ears at Na'jif, sunlight glinting off gold minarets that rose high above the ancient city's fortifications, her black skirt beginning to feel heavy and hot.

How could she tell him there *wasn't* an antidote—not one that had been tested on humans, anyway.

A wave of nausea churned through her. Dizziness spiraled her brain. "Please stop this camel!" she said quietly. "I...I...I'm going to be sick."

He reined the beast in and she slid immediately down from the saddle, misjudging the height and falling into a heap on the hot sand. She scrambled to her feet, took a few steps away from him, and clutched her arms over her stomach. She stared over dunes that undulated in an unending ocean of yellows and golds and browns all the way to a blinding horizon. She couldn't run; there was nowhere to go. Her stomach heaved violently. She bent over, clutched tighter.

She didn't want to hear anymore.

She simply could not absorb the scope of what he was saying. It didn't make any sense. Could Nexus really be making bioweapons, using the other quadrants as fronts—or just using the research of innocent scientists like herself?

Had they illegally tested her pathogens on innocent people?

Had she been a pawn all this time? Could she really have been this naive for not having seen or suspected something?

Another wave of nausea rode hard through her body. She gripped her stomach again and heaved. Her muscles cramped in pain, but nothing came up. She caught her breath, stood slowly, waited until her head felt a little more steady.

What if it was all a lie? What if the Silent Revolution did have an informant at the Nexus compound? What if they wanted to use her pathogen to attack the sultan and his army? *That* could be why they needed the antidote. They might want to contain a biological attack. It could be done, if they were properly prepared. There would still be casualties, but...

She turned suddenly, glared at him perched high and arrogant on his camel. "I don't believe you!" she yelled. She just couldn't. "It's a lie! I think you want my work for your *own* reasons!" She pointed at his face. "You bear the mark of a rebel—"

His patience snapped.

In one fluid movement he swung his camel toward her. Hooves barreled towards her as he lunged down, grabbed her arm, hauled her roughly back up into the saddle.

Paige screamed in shock.

He kicked his beast into a fast gallop as she groped wildly, trying to hold on as her body beat against the animal's and her skirt flapped at her ankles. He did nothing to help her.

She managed to maneuver herself up, grasp hold of the saddle horn, pull herself upright, totally out of breath. "You *bastard!*" she hissed.

He put his mouth to her ear and growled low. "You know what, Doctor? I don't believe *you* either."

Chapter 4

Rafiq was now certain that Paige Sterling was the mastermind behind the pathogen. But he didn't know what else to believe about her. Maybe she really didn't know anything about the true nature of Nexus.

Or maybe she was bluffing.

Didn't matter either way. They'd soon have full access to the Nexus computers and all of her work. Once the download was complete, his phase of this mission was over. The medical team in the Level 4 lab they'd set up on São Diogo could get busy analyzing the data, and he could get the hell out of this country.

He'd never intended to come back here. Ever. And the sooner he was out, the better. For everyone. Each minute he remained on Hamānian soil was a minute too long, and an increased risk. If his true identity was discovered, the whole country would blow.

And this mission would fail.

Not even his FDS colleagues knew the depth of his history here. Rafiq drew his turban back over his face as they neared the walls of Na'jif. He looked like any Bedouin nomad now. And Paige Sterling was going to look like any Bedouin wife once he had her kitted out in a proper *chador* and jewelry.

He leaned forward. "Keep that scarf over your face now." He spoke into her neck, and it sent a small shudder through her body. He smiled slightly.

The cool scientist was not beyond reacting to him, and the notion pleased him in a purely male way. He closed his eyes for a moment. She was an inconvenience, one he would abandon as soon as they crossed the border. But it didn't mean he couldn't enjoy her physical proximity. Or her beauty. The scientist was damn sexy when she got all fired up.

And when those stormy gray eyes started flashing… He suspected they just might be his downfall if he wasn't careful.

Foot traffic increased as they neared the city gates. An old truck piled high with hay clattered along the road, leaving desert dust and diesel fumes in its wake. Paige coughed, pressed her scarf over her nose and mouth as it passed. It wasn't even eight in the morning and already the heat was brutal. It made her body hot and damp against his, lifting her scent into the air. He guided his camel around a man bent over a rusty bicycle.

Paige stared at the man and muttered something.

Rafiq's pulse accelerated slightly—it sounded as if she'd said there was *no* antidote. He leaned forward. "*What* was that you said?"

But she sat silent.

"Paige?"

She shook her head. "It…it was nothing," she said quietly.

But it bothered him. There *had* to be an antidote—a whole stockpile somewhere. The Cabal simply would not risk what they were doing without a means to control the outcome.

They entered the thick stone walls of Na'jif and the din of the city engulfed them, making conversation impossible.

He'd have to wait until they got back to the apartment before he interrogated her further. And the Nexus computers would tell them what they needed regardless of what he'd thought he'd heard her say.

He wove his camel through the throngs of people heading for the market, an historic trading center at the city center where one day's sales were said to have equaled one month's in Cairo back in the Middle Ages.

He pulled the reins sharply to avoid a fruit cart that rumbled over the cobblestones. An apple bounced off the back and rolled into the street. Two small boys laughed, let go of their mother's skirts and chased it, ducking between carts and the legs of camels. The vignette grabbed Rafiq by the throat.

He slowed, turned to watch them, and a deep and painful nostalgia swelled through his chest. He and Nahla had hoped to have children. They'd talked about it while walking in these very streets.

Rafiq sucked his breath in sharply at the sudden and visceral nature of the memory, and he killed the thought instantly. But it was too late. The damage was done—an old scar had ripped open, and now the hollow pain was back, lingering like low smoke trapped in a canyon, a pain he'd managed to quash for well over a decade.

Rafiq swore to himself as he negotiated a mound of garlic piled almost six feet high at the entrance to a narrow alley. He'd misjudged his emotional fortitude. Coming back was going to be tougher than he'd anticipated.

As they drew closer to the market square, the scents and sounds grew richer. Even through the fabric of his head-cloth, Rafiq could smell tomatoes warmed by hot sun, salted fish, bergamot, lemons. Another cart rattled past them, this one stacked with bundles of mildly narcotic qat from the lowlands near Yemen. The local men still clearly loved to chew the leaves. Little had changed in fifteen years, yet much was different.

As they moved deeper into the warren of city streets, Rafiq had to admit, as much as he'd tried to block it all out, as much distance and time as he'd tried to put between himself and his past, this place—its scents and rhythms—was still in his blood. It was still a part of who he was.

He turned his camel into the wide main street, and a giant portrait of Sultan Sadiq bin Zafir bin Omar al-Qaadr blazed into his vision.

Rafiq jerked the camel to a stop, glared up at the image of the Scarred Sultan, oblivious suddenly to the throngs around him and to the woman seated in front of him.

The portrait hung right over the middle of the street, dominating the thoroughfare. And whoever had been commissioned to paint it had omitted the vicious puckered scar that Rafiq knew marred the man's throat.

The scar *he'd* put there.

His fists clenched the reins and bitterness leached into his mouth as the sweet image of Nahla swam into his brain. Raw aggression spiked his blood and Rafiq's eyes went hot. *No!*

He blinked it away.

He did not want to relive those memories. And now that he was actually back in Na'jif, he could see he was in trouble. He cursed bitterly. Just one sight of Sadiq's image and his fingers were itching for his scimitar. He had to finish the damn download and get the hell out this country ASAP, before he did—or said—something he'd regret.

He clenched his teeth, jerked the reins, and kicked his camel forward and down into a tiny alleyway where the buildings on either side loomed so close they strangled the sun.

Paige stood in the alley holding the camel's head rope. Rafiq had left her and the smelly beast waiting outside a tiny stockroom with Persian rugs stacked high behind murky windows. Even alone in the streets with a means of transport in her hands, she was still trapped. She wouldn't make it beyond the city walls without the Land Command being alerted. She knew they had paid informants everywhere—usually peasants so desperate for cash or favor they were willing to snitch on fellow countrymen who defied the sultan's orders.

She pulled her scarf higher over her face, aware that she was garnering suspicious looks from the few passersby in this dark lane.

She shifted her weight from one foot to the other as the minutes seemed to tick by interminably and perspiration trickled slowly down between her breasts. She had no idea what the time was, and the scent of sweet pastry coming from the bakery next door was making her stomach twist in hunger. She was thirsty, too—for an ice-cold lemonade. Come to think of it, plain old water from a goatskin bag would do just fine.

How could she be thinking of food now?

She'd just been told that the work she'd devoted her entire life to was being used to threaten the most powerful nation on this earth. She was theoretically dead to the Western world, completely at the mercy of a dangerously enigmatic mercenary in a land as old and mysterious as time…and here she was wanting *pastry?*

How was a woman supposed to react to all this, anyway? She shifted her weight again, her knee throbbing from her fall earlier. Why did she even have to *think* about how to react? Why did she have to analyze everything? Couldn't she just react from her heart and gut like normal people?

What *was* normal, anyway?

She'd spent way too much of her life in a Level 4 lab to know what was "normal." And before that, she'd been homeschooled in the wilds of places like the Congo jungle and Papua, New Guinea. She understood primitive tribes and wildlife better than she understood her peers.

Her stomach growled again as another wave of warm, sweet scent drifted her way, and hunger once again took precedence over her thoughts.

The camel jerked suddenly against his rope and peeled back fat lips exposing yellow overlapping incisors. Paige eyed his teeth warily. The beast was also getting impatient. She'd take a horse over one of these gnarly creatures any day. She tried to edge farther away from his teeth while still maintaining her hold on his rope. The animal grunted in protest. Next he was going to spit at her, she was sure of it. He had that look in his eyes.

A breath of relief flew out of her as she saw Rafiq reappear in the doorway of the carpet store. This was not good—she was actually relieved to see her captor. Paige tried to tell herself it was natural—she was just scared and she was dependent on this man. For now.

It had nothing to do with his glorious dark looks, or powerful magnetism. Or the way he'd made her feel on the ride across the desert.

Rafiq exited the store and strode toward her with a stocky man at his side—probably the carpet dealer, Paige thought. He was dressed in a white robe and traditional red-and-white checkered head cloth. A ring of keys hung from a chain at his waist, and he walked with an air of authority. She guessed he was a boss of some sort, someone with status in Na'jif.

He stopped in front of her, appraised her with eyes as dark and shiny as the black prayer beads he was rolling between his fingers. She stared defiantly back at him before realizing she should probably avert her eyes if she wanted to avoid trouble, at least while they were out in public.

She slanted her eyes toward the ground as the carpet dealer selected a large key from his chain and slotted it into the wrought-iron gate that closed off a dark and narrow passage that ran between the bakery and the carpet shop. He creaked the heavy black gate open, motioned for her and Rafiq to enter. Paige hesitated, unsure of what to do with the camel.

"Bring him," said Rafiq stepping through the gateway ahead of her.

She swallowed a spike of irritation. This was *his* camel, not hers. But she said nothing as she led the protesting beast through the gate.

She followed the two men down the alley. It was surprisingly cool inside the thick whitewashed stone walls. As her eyes adjusted to the darkness, Paige could make out a large courtyard up ahead. A stable ran along the far end, and there was a pile of fresh hay in the middle. They entered the courtyard and a young boy immediately ran forward to take the camel from her. She handed it over with relief.

Rafiq and the dealer had moved over to a secluded corner and were conversing in the local dialect in tones too low for her to pick up. They both glanced up at her—obviously discussing her. And this time she declined to look away, refusing to be treated like some second-rate citizen not worthy of an introduction or inclusion in their conversation. It was then that she noticed Rafiq, while still keeping his Tuareg-style turban wound over his mouth, had let the cloth drop just enough to expose the tattoo on his cheekbone. Paige's heart quickened.

She flicked her eyes over the carpet dealer, trying to gauge his reaction to the tattoo. To her surprise, she saw that he too sported a sign of the Silent Revolution. At the open neck of his robe was a leather thong and on it dangled a tiny gold scimitar—the stylized symbol of the scimitar the true king had used to slice the neck of his older brother Sadiq before fleeing the country, never to return.

Paige frowned. So the Silent Revolution wasn't so silent here in Na'jif. This had to be some kind of safe house, a nerve center of the underground struggle. But if Rafiq was happy to show his tattoo, why was he still hiding the rest of his face?

The dealer said something and Rafiq nodded. Then he strode over to her, took her hand in his, possessively, affectionately. This startled Paige. So did the warm, electrical sensation of his skin against hers. He drew her closer to himself, his eyes warning her not to resist.

He must have told the dealer they were a couple. And

she hadn't even thought of resisting. The sense of contact, affection, even if fake, was actually welcome in this strange and hostile environment. What in heavens was wrong with her? Stockholm Syndrome, that's what it was called. She was bonding with her captor—her lifeline. She tried to convince herself that her reactions were perfectly understandable.

Rafiq led her out of the courtyard, through a narrow arch-covered walkway and up a set of twisting stone stairs. At the top he unlocked a heavy wood door, opening it out onto the domed entrance area of an exotic rooftop apartment.

He ushered her in, and locked the door behind them. Paige watched him pocket the key in his tunic. She noted the door was heavily reinforced with ironwork. Sun streamed through the stained glass dome above them, dappling them with oranges and reds and greens.

To the left was a tiled passage leading to what looked like the living quarters. Rafiq motioned for her to move to the right and out onto a rooftop courtyard.

Paige caught her breath as she stepped into the blinding sunshine.

The view of the ancient city that stretched below the courtyard parapets was breathtaking. Minarets and mosques gleamed gold in the sun, and she could make out the marketplace in the distance, a wide square area that teemed with shimmering movement and color. "What is this place?" she whispered in awe.

"Belongs to a Na'jif merchant. He's away on business and I'm renting it for the week."

She turned full circle, taking it all in. The air was thick with the scent of jasmine growing in earthenware pots and trailing up ornate trellises. A small fountain splashed into a mosaic birdbath, and under an area covered with a canvas awning sat furniture upholstered with rich brocades.

Then she saw the Halliburton case.

It rested on an ornately carved dark wood desk. Next to it was what looked like sophisticated communications equipment—a rare and very dangerous sight in a country where even the possession of a phone was illegal. She glanced at Rafiq. He was watching her intently, an inscrutable look in his dark eyes.

"What is that stuff?"

"My equipment." He pointed. "That's a satellite transmitter over there. Computer is in the case."

"Is that what you were doing at Nexus? Installing a wireless uplink for download?"

He nodded. "We plan to capture the entire system, relay the information back to the São Diogo base. Once the download is complete, we move out of Hamān. We've set up a Level 4 lab on the island, and we have a team of top scientists on standby to interpret the information. It would help, Paige, if you told us up front where Nexus and BioMed may have stockpiled vaccines."

Horror filled her. She knew nothing about vaccine stockpiles. She glanced at him, then back at the equipment. "You…you never intended to kidnap me, did you?"

"No." He twisted his turban off as he spoke. "Didn't expect anyone to be in the lab at that hour."

"So I was just a loose end?"

"Correct." He tossed his turban over the back of a chair, began to untie the belts at his waist. "Couldn't leave you there. And couldn't kill you—you're a key player."

"Would you have…*killed* me otherwise?"

He didn't respond. He lifted the black tunic over his

head, tossed it onto the chair with his turban, and raked his fingers loosely through his dark hair. It was so black it almost had a blue gleam to it, and it fell to his shoulders in loose waves. He was wearing a white T-shirt that showed every rippling muscle of his rock-hard frame and offset the duskiness of his skin.

She lowered her eyes nervously, watching his hands as he resecured his dagger to his waist. She noted he also sported a handgun in a leather holster at his hips. That was something he wouldn't have wanted the Land Command to find, either. She looked up at his face, at his tattoo.

This man was a walking affront to the sultan.

And he was capable of killing her.

If he had complete access to the Nexus computers and a team of scientists to interpret the data, he would soon see that she was completely useless to him, that she had nothing to do with weaponizing the pathogen, that she had no knowledge of any antidote stockpiles.

With a sinking feeling, Paige realized she would then probably be completely dispensable. The only reason she was alive right now was because he thought she might know something.

She had to pretend she did if she wanted a bargaining tool, if she wanted to get out of Hamān alive. Otherwise she had nothing. And he had no reason to keep her.

She closed her eyes for a moment, trying to gather her fear. "And the carpet dealer?" she asked softly. "Who is he?"

"Landlord," he said as he strode over to the desk, flipped open the Halliburton case. "We stay here until the Nexus computer system is uplinked and the download complete." He pulled out an aerial and began to link wires.

Paige just stared.

"This will take a while," he said without looking at her. "Bathroom and bedrooms are back through the entrance hall and to the left. I've ordered food."

Her stomach rumbled again. She placed her hand over it, moved over to the chaise lounge, sat gingerly on the end. She watched him put bits and pieces of equipment together and noted in some distant part of her brain that he had strong, eloquent fingers. He tweaked a few dials and static suddenly crackled. Her heart skipped a beat.

They were now linked to the rest of the world. She leaned closer, trying to see exactly what he was doing.

A knock sounded at the door.

Paige jerked back in shock as Rafiq lurched to his feet, grabbing his black headcloth and flinging it over his face in one deft movement, leaving only his eyes and tattoo exposed. He fished the key from his tunic pocket. "Stay there," he barked as he strode to the entrance area. She heard the key slot into the door, and the creak of iron hinges as it opened.

She heard a female voice. Then a woman, old and bent, carrying a tray of food tried to enter around the side of the trellis. Rafiq muttered something and took the tray from her, not permitting her to come into the courtyard area. The woman tried to peer round him, overtly curious about the foreign female visitor in his quarters. Paige noticed she was nervously fingering a locket that dangled from a chain at her waist.

The three women who did the laundry at the Nexus residential compound carried lockets like that. Theirs held blurry replicas of an old photograph of the young true sultan taken shortly before he'd fled Hamān more than fifteen years ago.

They'd shown their lockets to Paige in confidence after

she'd been friendly with them for nearly two years. They'd told her in hushed and reverent tones that the *real* king would one day return to save them from the oppressive rule of the Scarred Sultan. They said many women in their villages hid lockets like this under their *chadors*. It was a risk because images of the young heir had been outlawed. But those images were also a symbol of hope.

It was strange what hope could do to people, because there was no way their true king was coming to save them. He was dead and buried.

Yet somehow they still believed, their story and their hero growing to mythical proportions over the years.

Paige wondered if this woman's locket held a similar grainy image, if she clung to the same dream. She guessed she did.

Paige heard the door close, and she heard him lock it. He came round the trellis carrying the tray. It held a bowl of red grapes, two tall glasses of mint tea, flatbreads, shaved lamb, and a bowl of yogurt sauce. Her mouth began to water.

He set the food on the glass-topped table in front of her before tossing off his turban again. She watched him slip the key back into his tunic pocket as she reached for the bunch of grapes. She plucked several off and popped them into her mouth.

She closed her eyes, crushing them with her teeth. Sweet juice cooled her throat. *Oh God, these were good.* She opened her eyes, reached for more, and felt him watching.

She stilled, lifted her eyes slowly to his. Her heart began to race.

Could *this* be her ticket out of Hamān, to staying alive? She studied his eyes, trying to read him, her body growing warm under his scrutiny. He might be sexually attracted to her, but somehow she doubted he'd allow himself to be manipulated that way.

And it was not her style—she wasn't sure if she could pull it off. She was physically attracted to him herself. Engaging him would be like touching fire; she might not be able to control the blaze.

She looked away, at the grapes, suddenly nervous. "Would…would you like some?" She picked up the bowl, held it out to him. "They really are good."

A muscle twitched along his mouth. "I'm sure they are," he said darkly.

Heat flushed her skin. She had to change the subject. Fast.

Paige cleared her throat, set the grapes very carefully back on the glass table. "You obviously trust them."

"Who?" His voice was husky, sending a shiver down her spine.

She swallowed, tried to focus on something other than his mouth. "The…the carpet dealer, and that woman. You let them see your tattoo. You're a rebel and you don't mind flaunting it to them."

"The tattoo washes off," he said brusquely and stalked back to the desk.

"What?"

"I said it washes off." He sat at the desk, his back to her, began to fiddle with his equipment.

"So you're faking it? It's just part of your cover?"

He said nothing.

Her brain reeled.

Know your enemy, Paige. Knowledge is power.

"Why…why would you pretend allegiance to the Silent Revolution?" she asked.

"Paige," he muttered as he untwisted wires, "don't you ever stop with the questions?"

Irritation spiked in her. "I wouldn't have to ask if you were up front with me."

He ignored her.

She grabbed another handful of grapes, stuffed them into her mouth as she poked at possible explanations. How would posing as a rebel serve a foreign mercenary, if that's really what he was? Obviously he wanted to avail himself of the underground network. It was virtually impossible for a foreigner to get into Hamān, let alone move through the country undetected, without being protected by the network. That could explain how he got the fake papers, how he managed to secure a camel, rent this place. He would not have been able to do it without some kind of local help.

"So you're using them."

He turned slowly in his chair, narrowed his focus on her. "That's right." She heard a warning in his voice.

Paige thought of the hope in the eyes of the women at the compound. "What did you tell them?"

"That I'm a returning exile, that I have access to funding and offshore contacts willing to supply weapons to their rebellion."

"You're giving them false hope?"

His brows lowered. "What's it to you?"

"Do you even begin to understand the depth and desperation of these people, Rafiq? Do you know how many years they've waited for a sign, for the return of their rightful king?"

He clenched his fists and stood so fast that his chair crashed back onto the tiles.

Paige shrank back in shock.

What was this? Had she just found an emotional chink in the mercenary's armor?

He walked slowly toward her, fire burning in his black eyes. He crouched down at her feet, lowering his eyes to her level. Hot energy rode off him in waves.

"How can an American scientist living on a guarded American compound know all this?"

She was nervous but met his glare head-on. The air crackled between them. A horn sounded down in the street. Lute music wafted in from a rooftop nearby.

She leaned slightly forward, heart thudding, and she spoke low and soft. "I know this, Rafiq, because I got to know the local people who worked on the compound. I've lived there for five years, and during that time I got to know the women who washed our clothes, cooked our food and dreamed of freedom. I got to know them so well, that they opened up to me, taught me their language. And they told me of their dream. I understand that dream, Rafiq, better than a hired mercenary ever could. You not only betray these people with your deceit, you *endanger* their lives."

Pain twisted through his features so fleetingly she thought she might have imagined it. He jerked back to his feet, glared down at her.

"This mission is bigger than Hamān," he snapped. "The *entire* world will suffer if the Cabal topples the U.S. government. These guys are imperialistic capitalists. If they take control of the White House they will kill democracy. They will launch an era of aggressive expansionism designed to bolster their global assets, and they will use weapons like those created in *your* lab, Paige."

He paused, his eyes searing hers. "This is bigger than

you. Or me. Or some Hamānian legend. This, Paige, is quite literally about saving the world."

She'd unleashed something in him, a mad kind of passion she couldn't quite fathom. She wondered just how far she could push him, and what she might learn if she did.

"You might want to save the world, Rafiq, but these people know little about that world. All they want is to save themselves. All they want is a future without Sadiq. And their underground network is fragile. If they're under the misguided belief you have brought support and weapons, they may become bold. You might force them to tip their hand. A breach like this could *kill* them."

She looked up at him, trying to hold herself steady in spite of her thumping heart, in spite of the ferocity crackling in his eyes. "I'm sure they'd kill to prevent that, Rafiq. I'm sure they'd hate to find out you're a fraud."

He stared at her, his eyes dark, unreadable. "Is that a threat, Doctor?"

"It's the truth."

And yes, a threat.

Paige finally had a bargaining tool, and damned if she wasn't going to use it.

Chapter 5

Rafiq's eyes glittered with anger. "You—" he pointed his finger at her face "—have no right to judge *me*. You are the one who created this diabolical disease. You're the one who works for a Cabal corporation."

"That's not—"

He raised his hands. "Don't even begin to try and tell me that you had no idea what you were doing sitting in that guarded compound. It's a lab built on foreign soil, *specifically* to avoid U.S. legislation. You work for a corporation that pays hefty fees to the sultan—fees he uses to bolster his corrupt regime. You—" he wagged his index finger at her "—you are the one destroying dreams in Hamān, Paige. You are the one betraying your *own* country."

She lurched to her feet. "I am not! I told you I knew nothing about this alleged Cabal. I took the job at Nexus to do research and development—to develop cures so that the world will be ready when the next big epidemic hits. That's the Nexus mandate. And believe me, if we're sitting there manipulating the DNA of viruses, you can bet the enemy is, too. And what would you rather do? Sit around and wait until they release the next pandemic, or rely on a company like Nexus that has done all kinds of preemptive research and has vaccines?"

"That it sells for massive profit to desperate governments through its pharmaceutical subsidiaries?"

"So what? The whole damn pharmaceutical industry operates that way. And the reason we do the work in places like Hamān is because we can't do it back home. Our research makes people uncomfortable." She took a step toward him. "Steel can be used to make both plowshares and swords, Rafiq. The diseases we create at Nexus are not dangerous. It's not the steel that's dangerous. *It's the intent.*" She looked pointedly at his sheathed scimitar. "And if someone comes at you with a sword, you're going to be damn thankful you have one in *your* arsenal to fight back with."

His eyes drilled into hers. "You *honestly* believe this?"

She hesitated. Right now she really wasn't sure of anything anymore. "I used to."

She tried to look away but he gripped her jaw, forced her to look into his eyes. Fear rippled through her, and her eyes began to water.

Then he suddenly released her, spun round and strode to the edge of the parapet.

Paige felt her body slump. She told herself it was exhaustion, stress, but in spite of her show of bravado, he'd defeated her. In a few hours, this man had managed to shatter her notion of who she was, and what she did as a scientist.

And suddenly she felt lost.

Paige made her way shakily back to the chaise lounge. She sat, watching him stalk along the parapet.

Rafiq stopped and stared out over the city he'd once loved so much.

His nails bit into his palms. Who the hell did Paige Sterling think she was, anyway? How could she profess to care so much about *his* people, implying she cared more than he did, or *could*.

Hell, maybe she did.

The only reason he'd come back was because his hand had been forced. And now that he was here, guilt sliced into him like a scimitar, and it fueled the flame he hadn't realized still burned so fiercely in him.

He paced along the parapet, feeling her questioning eyes on his back, feeling the intense heat of direct sun on his head. Dr. Paige Sterling wasn't supposed to have righteous moral beliefs about her work. He hadn't anticipated this aspect of her personality when he'd seen her image and read her file in the FDS situation room.

He hadn't really bothered thinking about her at all. He wasn't supposed to have engaged her in any way.

And now here she was lecturing him about his own people.

God, he even respected her for it. She hadn't just been sitting in that ivory tower of a lab; she'd been out there, feet in the sand, getting to know the locals, learning the dialect. And if she really *was* telling the truth, if she *was* being used, he was obligated to go easy on her. To keep her safe.

Yet he was furious with her for slamming him in the face with what he'd chosen to ignore for the last fifteen years.

Because now he couldn't look away anymore. Now he was *obligated* to do something for his people

And he couldn't. His hands were tied.

He had to fulfill this mission or put millions of innocent lives at risk.

He stopped pacing, raked his hands through his hair. He couldn't afford to think about Paige or Hamān now—there was work to be done. And he was going to do it.

Rafiq stalked back to the desk and began to jab at the keyboard. He hit the Enter key and the satellite radio crackled to life. He hit another sequence of keys, ensuring encryption. A voice transcended distance. "*Sauvage ici.*"

"*C'est Rafiq.*"

"Zayed, are we in?"

He pressed another series of keys, hit Enter. "Yeah, we're in."

There was moment of silence as the satellite feed locked onto its target from the FDS base on São Diogo Island off the coast of Africa.

"*Bien.* I see the screen now. I'll get December and his crew started on the download ASAP. We'll know within 24 hours how long the process will take. It's going to depend on the encryption and pass codes, but we can start analyzing the data as soon as it begins to come through."

Rafiq glanced sideways at Paige. "There is just one other thing."

"What?"

"I have the doctor."

"What!"

"She was working in the lab and saw me. I couldn't leave her."

"What about the Cabal? Why haven't they reacted to her disappearance?"

"Made it look like she had an accident. Brake failure—car over the cliff."

"They won't find a body."

"The water off those cliffs is notoriously deep and full of hammerheads, and the currents swift. Even if there was a body, and even if they went looking, it might never be found under the circumstances. I think it'll hold."

Silence stretched. "We use her, then. She can help with access codes. It could speed the process considerably. I'll let you know what the techs need from her." He paused. "Do what it takes to get the information from her."

Rafiq signed off with an irritable jab at the keyboard and consulted his watch. All he could do right now was sit here, couped up in this apartment with Paige, watching the clock tick down on a global threat of incomprehensible proportion.

Waiting did not sit easy with Rafiq.

He sucked air in slowly, and he turned his thoughts beyond the download, to getting out of Hamān.

If he was going to take Paige with him, she would need a regulation *chador*. And they'd need another camel, more supplies.

He looked at her.

She'd removed her *hijab*, and her hair lay smooth, like pale moonlight, on her shoulders. Her eyes were fixed on him as she ate bread dipped in yogurt. She really was very attractive, in a cool and unattainable way. And too damn smart for her own good, with a mouth to match. Beauty, brains and a whole lot of pain in the ass, that's what she was.

He stood, strode over to the table in front of her, picked up a glass of tea. As he brought the glass to his lips he caught sight of the bloody nick on her neck, the skin going red around it. His hand froze mid-air.

He'd done that to her.

A sick sensation sunk through him. He took a deep drink and plunked his glass back on the table. "Finish your food," he said, more brusquely than he needed to. "We're going to the market. You need a *chador*."

She swallowed her mouthful and her eyes widened. "You're going to take me *with you?*"

"I'm not leaving you here with my equipment."

Her eyes flicked over to the desk. He could literally see her thinking, and he felt himself steeling for another verbal sparring session. He'd prefer to avoid that, prefer she kept that pretty mouth of hers shut, because he didn't like what kept coming out of it.

"You could tie me up," she offered.

"No," he said simply, but by God he'd like to. He could think of a couple of good reasons, and not all of them business-related.

"Why not? It didn't bother you before."

"You done eating yet?"

"You're worried that your rebel 'friends' might find me bound up in your apartment, is that it? You're afraid I'll tell them who you really are."

"Don't you *ever* stop asking questions?" he snapped.

"It's what I do for a living—ask questions. Then I find answers."

He donned his tunic, snagged his turban off the chair and began to wind the fabric over and around his head. He refused to allow her to engage him again.

"How did you explain me to the carpet dealer? Did you tell him we were married?"

"I told him you're my annoying American wife and that you're here to help us rebels. I told him the offshore money contacts were yours and that you wanted to see the situation in Hamān firsthand before authorizing the release of cash for weapons."

She fell silent.

He flipped the end of his turban over his shoulder, stepped right up close to her, toe to toe, forcing her to crick her neck to look up at him. "And think about this, Paige—*your* safe passage out of Hamān now depends on those people and their underground network. You're just as complicit as I in deceiving them. Blow my cover and you go down with me, I guarantee it."

"That *is* a threat."

"No, that, Dr. Sterling, really is the truth." He paused, letting his words sink in. "You done eating now?"

Her eyes flickered nervously. "Yes."

"Cover yourself, then, and let's go."

"I…I need to use the bathroom first."

He stepped back, jerked his head in the direction of the hallway. "Back through there and to your left." There was no way she could escape. He had the key to the main door. And they were three stories up.

She got to her feet stiffly, favoring one leg. Guilt twisted in him again. That was also his fault. He'd been pretty rough on her, and she was not a complainer. If she was hurting, she was hiding it from him. He should ask if she was okay.

But he couldn't bring himself to.

He watched her disappear behind the trellis as she went into the covered section of the apartment, and he made a mental note to bring it up later. Not because he cared, he told himself, but because an injury would hold them up when they made their run for the Saudi border. They'd have to head over a stretch of arid desert plain, and then up into the rough mountainous terrain of the Asir range. And they'd have to move fast, preferably at night. It wasn't going to be a trip for the faint of heart.

Rafiq checked that his firearm was securely hidden under his tunic, then he thrust the *jambiya* into the front of his belt. He reached for his scimitar as she reappeared in the archway. He looked up.

Her freshly-scrubbed skin was pink and her hair was tied back. It made her look young, more than a little vulnerable. Something spasmed through his heart. He tightened his jaw, roughly sheathed his scimitar.

He didn't have time for compassion, for feelings of tenderness. He'd managed to avoid feeling those things for all the women he dated and slept with over the past fifteen years. So why now? Why her?

He couldn't keep his physical attraction for her separate from emotion. This woman had a way of forcing the two to twist inextricably into one complex and threatening sensation. Rafiq had an uneasy—and fleeting—notion that he just might have met his match in Dr. Paige Sterling. And he'd probably do best if he put a cap on his lust.

Maybe he could avoid the emotion and guilt that way. He cleared his throat.

"You ready?"

She hesitated. Was that a flicker of fear in her eyes? He paid closer attention. "What is it, Paige?"

She bit her lip, the action strangely endearing. "It's nothing. It's okay. Let's go."

He grasped her arm, drew her slowly closer to him. "Paige, you need to talk to me."

She inhaled deeply, her eyes nervous. "I don't understand how this Cabal plans on taking over the government. And what if the president *does* step down in eleven days, just to buy time? We won't need the antidote then…will we?"

He frowned. "Paige," he said, his voice low, his hand still on her arm. "We *need* that antidote. No matter what."

Emotion glimmered in her eyes.

"Look, the president is not going to step down. He can't. He's dying, Paige. He has to hold on just long enough to win the election next month and stop Forbes from taking over. And we—"

"He's *dying?*"

"Yes. He's being slowly assassinated by a variation of one of the prion pathogens from *your* lab, Dr. Sterling." He watched her face carefully.

Her eyes widened, her mouth opened in shock. She shook her head. "I…I don't…what are his symptoms?"

"It looks like a rapid Alzheimer's, or dementia, according to his personal physician. But he's managed to hide it so far. He won't be able to do it for much longer, though. He's supposed to be dead already. Forbes was supposed to have taken over under the 25th Amendment long before this election. But the disease is obviously not working as fast as the Cabal had anticipated, and this is why they've issued the ultimatum for him to step down before he wins that election and secures a new term without Forbes as his veep."

Her face went sheet-pale. "Because if Elliot wins, which no one doubts he will, his running mate, Michael Taylor, will assume the presidency, *not* Forbes? Because Forbes was excluded from the Elliot ticket."

He nodded, his eyes intently watching hers.

She rubbed her hands over her face. "Forbes wasn't

elected in the first place," she said, more to herself than him. "He was appointed veep after Charles Landon died." Her eyes shot to his. "Why did Elliot appoint Forbes, then, if he was with the Cabal?"

"Landon didn't die a natural death, either, Paige. He was assassinated with a biological weapon. It was made to look natural. And Elliot had been told that he, too, had been infected with a biological bullet, only his death would be slower, giving him time to name Forbes as his second-in-command. He was told a plague would be unleashed on his people if he didn't. So he did. He named Forbes, but only to buy time to come up with a plan."

"And you are that plan."

"His last resort. And this ultimatum for him to stand down is now the Cabal's last resort. The Cabal has been positioning Forbes for years. They cannot afford to lose this small window of opportunity now."

"But why go to these lengths? Why don't they just kill Elliot quickly, shoot him or something, before the election?"

He angled his head. "You're a hard woman, Doctor."

Her eyes flashed wildly. "I'm trained to ask the hard questions, Rafiq."

He nodded slowly. "The Cabal needs his death to look like a natural illness. An overt assassination will raise too many questions, and it will undermine Forbes' hold on power, and it will jeopardize the Cabal's plans for the future. You see, Paige, once the Cabal has control of the White House, they will *still* release their bioweapons, only in smaller, more contained doses. There will *still* be civilian casualties. Forbes will allege that the nation is under attack by 'terrorists.' They will instill fear, cancel elections for the foreseeable future, and a terrified nation will rally behind their new man. They will grant their 'wartime' president sweeping powers that will obliterate civil liberties, and enable military 'retaliation' against the so-called rogue nations that harbor the alleged terrorists. Forbes in turn will begin the slow process of appointing Cabal members to key positions of power...you getting the picture yet?"

She couldn't speak. Her eyes were wide, glistening. "And...Landon's death...was it..."

"A prion illness? Yes, it was."

She tried to swallow.

His grip tightened on her arm. "*That* is why we need the antidote, Paige. *That* is why we must stop this Cabal before October 13. If we get the antidote in time, we might even just be able to save the president, along with his nation."

Paige sighed. "There is no antidote, Rafiq."

He clenched his jaw. He'd suspected she was going to say this. "There has to be," he said quietly.

"There isn't. At least, *I* haven't created anything that has been tested on humans. In primates, yes, but—"

"The Cabal would *never* risk this without being able to control it."

Tears filled her eyes. She was ghostly white now, and trembling slightly under his fingers. She shook her head, and the tears spilled down her cheeks. Rafiq's heart twisted sharply.

"Oh, God," she whispered. "I...I never meant to create anything...like this. I..."

He couldn't help it. He moved instinctively from combat to comfort mode, gathering her into his arms and holding her against his chest, stroking her hair as her tears dampened his shoulder. Her hair was like liquid silk under his fingers, and her skin was soft. Her scent filled his lungs, and Rafiq knew he was done for.

Whether he believed her or not.

14:00 Charlie, Venturion Tower, Manhattan, Thursday, October 2

"It was an unfortunate accident. Her brakes failed and she went over the cliffs at around 2 a.m. Hamānian time." He rolled his silver pen tightly between his fingers as he scrutinized the faces of the men seated around the table. He'd called his board together to brief them on the "incident" that had occurred at their Nexus compound just twelve hours ago.

"Have they found her body yet?" The question came from the youngest member of the group, a sharp and cynical man who'd been brought into the inner sanctum only recently.

"No. Looking for a body would involve bringing in a team of U.S. divers. I don't believe that would be the best use of our resources at the moment, and we certainly can do without attracting any media or government attention at this critical juncture."

"Her family will expect us to at least attempt retrieval. Their protests alone could draw attention."

He considered the man, then turned to look at the other board members. Face by face he studied them, tomorrow's leaders. He'd known nearly every one of them for the last forty years, since their university days. They'd grown together, and their collective dream had taken shape over the decades. These men were his empire, and when they were gathered together like this, he could literally taste the power they wielded.

"She has no kin," he said, carefully skirting the issue

of her parents' murder. "Our surveillance has shown that she has no intimate friendships, either. She's a true loner. This is, of course, what made her so incredibly suitable for our purposes."

He laid his pen down and steepled his fingers. "Thankfully, her job is basically complete. We have no further need of her."

"I don't like it." This came from the youngest of the group again. "What if she escaped? Maybe she got wind of what was going on, got scared, took off."

"And where would she go? The borders in Hamān are closed. Women can't travel alone. Journalists are banned. Foreigners are not welcome. Anyone out of place is viewed with extreme suspicion, arrested and investigated by the Land Command—all reasons we stationed the Nexus complex there in the first place."

"What if she was taken?"

"Taken?"

"Kidnapped, abducted. I mean, we had this thing go wrong in the Congo, that nurse escaping with the pathogen. If Dr. Sterling was abducted—"

"There's no evidence of that." He got to his feet, asserting his authority.

He didn't like anything about this situation, either, but he was not going to waver in front of the board. Not now. Not with the deadline only eleven days away. He could not afford any fissures in the group's *absolute* confidence that their plan would succeed. Fear bred fear. Thoughts of failure led to failure. He placed both hands firmly on the table and leaned on them. "If we learn *anything* to the contrary, we will release the pathogen instantly." He forced a smile. "Thank you, gentlemen."

He pushed open the boardroom door, effectively calling the meeting to a close, and he made straight for his private office.

He opened his drawer, removed a secure cell phone, the one he used only to contact his cleanup man. He pressed the speed dial.

"Yes?"

"I need a job done. Where are you?"

Silence.

He shifted in his seat. His hit man was one of the few people in this world who could make him nervous. The guy was a psychopath, but a damn useful one. "I'm only asking because I need you somewhere fast."

"I'm in the Sudan."

Relief surged through him. His man was still in Africa. With the right papers and transport, he could be in place within hours. "I have something else for you—in Hamān."

"I'm listening."

"There's been an accidental death—an employee at the Nexus compound in Hamān. It's one of our outfits. I need you to make sure there actually is a body, and I want to know more about how she died. Tell no one why you're there. I'll secure entry permits with the sultan himself. To the locals, you're a bureaucrat looking for expansion opportunities on behalf of the Nexus Research and Development Corporation. To Nexus staff, you're an insurance investigator. I'll make sure you have full cooperation and full security clearance."

Silence.

The man was not a talker. He even refused to give updates. There would be no contact with him after this call until the job was done. Not knowing the status of the job was the price paid for the effectiveness of this man's services.

He cleared his throat. "I'll forward specifics via our e-mail drop."

"And if there is no body?"

"You find out why, and who helped her, and then you make sure there is one." He hung up, sank back into his chair. He didn't like this at all. Not after the Congo incident.

He told himself it was fine. He'd taken care of things in the Congo, and he'd take care of this, too. His hit man was uncanny, almost inhuman. He hadn't let him down yet.

If Dr. Paige Sterling was still alive, she wasn't going to stay that way for long.

Chapter 6

Awnings and wooden stands stretched in a brightly colored patchwork as far as Paige could see. All around her people jostled for position at stalls, bargaining fast and furious—the men wearing everything from gold-trimmed robes and bright brocades to rough burlap, women floating like black ghosts among them, leaving only perfumed scent and mystery in their wake.

Paige pulled her headscarf more firmly over her blond hair, making sure it was pinned securely across her nose and mouth. She was scared, and she was out of her depth—in more ways than one. At least her clothes were black. Maybe no one would notice her in the overwhelming chaos of this place.

Rafiq took her hand. "Stand around like that and you stick out like a beacon," he whispered against her ear as he led her right into the bustling commercial heart of Na'jif. "We need to keep moving."

She clung firmly to Rafiq. Without him, she was lost. This was *not* a place for someone who appreciated personal space or the solitude of a Level 4 lab and hazmat suit. But in spite of herself, the excitement of the place began to override her senses, the rich sounds and scents layered in the desert heat sweeping her exhausted mind to a state where she couldn't even begin to think of her lab, the pathogens, the president of the United States, or the fact that she might be indirectly responsible for trying to assassinate him. *Or* the fact that she'd broken down in front of her captor, and he'd held her in a way so tender and so sensual that it seemed he actually cared for her.

No one had held her like that in years. She hadn't broken down like that in front of anyone, either, not since she was fifteen…since she lost her parents.

It made Paige realize just how isolated she'd kept herself over the years—how she'd used her lab and her science as barriers. Because she was afraid of being hurt, of being left alone.

She knew she'd completely shut down emotionally after her experience in the jungle. It was the only way she'd managed to keep going on her own after her parents went missing that terrible night—after all the Congolese porters had fled, save one. That man had managed to get her out of the darkest jungle known to man. It had taken them more than two weeks to find civilization again. When she came out she'd been deathly ill, covered in leeches and forever changed—her heart locked away. It had affected her relationships ever since.

But this place, this exotic man, the fact that the old Paige Sterling was supposed to be dead to the world—those were all breaking down those psychological barriers, liberating her in a strange—and frightening—way.

Rafiq drew her deeper and deeper into the rich labyrinth of people and stalls and sounds and scents until Paige felt as if she'd been physically drawn back through the ages.

She found herself standing in front of a stall with row upon row of mysterious glass vessels stoppered with corks, some of them decorated with pewter or silver.

The woman behind the stall pulled a cork from the neck of a tall, slender bottle and held it out for Paige. Her dark eyes twinkled through the slit in her veil, inviting her to sample her wares. Paige leaned forward, sniffed. The fragrance was heady with notes of frankincense, bergamot and orange oil. She really liked it. She pointed to another bottle, but just as the woman was about to pull out the stopper, Rafiq yanked her back and forced her back into the teeming throng of people.

"What the—"

"Keep your head down," he hissed in Arabic. "Here, put this on, quick." He held out a large triangle of folded black cloth. Paige had been so strangely lost in the ambience of the ancient market she hadn't even seen him buying the *chador*. Her eyes shot to his in surprise. "You want me to put it on *here?*"

"Right now. And no English!"

"What's happening?"

"*Land Command,*" he whispered in Arabic. "Hurry!"

She looked up, saw a cadre of soldiers on horses

entering the northern entrance of the square. Panic gripped her. People were parting around them like waves, a hushed warning rippling through the crowd ahead of them.

Perspiration prickled her skin. She fumbled with the cloth, dropped it, picked up, yanked it over her head, tried to straighten it out over her clothing.

The Land Command came closer.

She frantically fiddled with the garment, trying to adjust the fabric so that she could see out the opening for the eyes. She got it into position and peered through the slit at Rafiq. All she could see of his face was his black eyes. And now that's all he could see of hers—eyes to eyes. They took on a new level of communication. In his, she could read not fear, not urgency, but a quiet burning rage. It was something she hadn't noticed before.

For a nanosecond, that dark and primal expression in his jet-black eyes made her forget her fear, but it kicked back the instant he looked away from her face and down at her hands.

She glanced down, realized instantly what he was seeing—pale skin, with none of the traditional rings and bracelets the local women wore. She yanked them back under her garment just as a soldier on horseback approached.

The soldier moved right next to her, his horse's hooves clacking over cobblestones. He slowed. Her pulse quickened. Then his horse snorted and Paige jerked back, her nerves already shot. The suddenness of her movement caught the soldier's attention. He stopped, ran his eyes slowly over her.

Her heart jackhammered. She averted her eyes, stared hard at the blackened cobblestones. But the soldier didn't move. Time stretched. Perspiration dampened her chest.

Still he didn't move. Raw fear strangled breath from her chest, squeezing logic right out of her brain. Paige was so used to maintaining mental control that the sheer terror of suddenly losing it compounded the violence of her reaction. Every molecule in her body screamed for her to flee even as she tried to force herself to stay still.

Then she felt Rafiq's hand under her *chador,* seeking hers. She clasped it quickly. It was firm, solid, an anchor. Relief punched through her and emotion welled sharply through her body.

She held on to him tighter, and her mind began to clear. She needed this man right now. How could he feel so right when everything was so wrong?

He squeezed her hand reassuringly, and she slid her eyes cautiously up to meet his, acutely aware of the Land Command officer still looming over her like a shadow.

Rafiq gestured with a small movement of his eyes that they move to the left. She closed her eyes briefly in acknowledgment, and he led her calmly back into the crowd.

Rafiq kept a check on the Land Command as he moved Paige well into the crowd. The soldiers had split into several groups and were working their way through the market stalls. They eventually stationed themselves in small groups at all four main entrances to the market square.

Why? Had someone alerted them? Or was this routine procedure? Whatever it was, he and Paige were going to have to pass them again on their way out. And she wasn't ready to pass the test. Yet.

He placed his hand at the small of Paige's back and steered her toward a cluster of small stalls wedged into a shadowed stone alcove at the very back of the square. She moved without resistance, responsive to the slightest pressure of his fingers.

She was clearly terrified and was trusting him to protect her. It nourished the male in him. And it heightened his desire for her. Her reminded himself of the need to keep her at a distance, knowing at the same time it was not going to be possible. Not after he'd held her like that.

He led her up to a table laden with local cosmetics and silver jewelry. Paige shot him a questioning look, her pale eyes even more startlingly beautiful framed by the black veil.

He squeezed her hand again. "Trust me," he whispered.

He greeted the woman behind the table and pointed to some sticks of kohl, packets of henna, several ankle chains and two loops of bracelets. She began to wrap his selections in a piece of indigo cloth, but he held up his hand, gesturing that she should wait. He glanced over his shoulder quickly, turned back and lowered the fabric of his head cloth away from his cheek.

The woman didn't even blink at the sight of his tattoo. She just nodded, her eyes fixed steadily on his.

Rafiq leaned forward over the table. "Can you do her hands and feet, and her eyes?" he asked, his voice low.

The woman didn't hesitate. She picked up the henna packets and a stick of black kohl, and held a wrinkled hand out to Paige.

Paige stiffened.

Rafiq nudged her forward. "Go with her. She's one of us, she won't say anything about your skin color, and by the time she's done, no one will notice anything different either."

Her eyes searched his. "You sure?"

"Of course I'm sure."

"How…how do you know she's *safe?*" she whispered.

"She was at the carpet dealer's house. Now, go. And here, take these, put them on when she's done." He flipped the cloth over the jewelry, handed her the parcel, and he watched the old woman lead his captive to a chair hidden behind a white bolt of canvas. There was no way Paige was going to blow his cover now. She was in just as deep as he was.

Rafiq browsed over the tables as he waited for Paige, the sun warm on his back, the sounds of the market stirring dormant synapses in his brain, awakening old pleasurable memories, linking them to the present. He realized with sudden shock that he was humming, an ancient Hamānian tune he hadn't thought of in years. It stopped him dead in his tracks.

A cocktail of emotion churned through him. Shopping at the Na'jif market with a woman—a woman he was actually beginning to care about—was tugging at sensations that he'd buried somewhere deep in his soul.

He used to come to this market with Nahla. He used to hold her hand as they browsed through these stalls, and he would look into her expressive dark eyes and dream of the day they would marry, and make love. The day he would make her his queen—Queen of Hamān.

Hot anger speared through his memories. He gripped the side of a table with both hands, trying to ground himself, trying to stay only in the present.

But coming back to this place with a woman at his side was like stepping right back into the past. It was cracking through the emotional armor he'd barricaded himself behind for the last fifteen years, releasing the volatile side of his nature—the side that got him into trouble, the side that could love as passionately and obsessively as it could hate.

Rafiq cursed violently under his breath.

This was *now*. This about his mission. This was *not* about him or his past. He was a soldier of fortune. He fought the battles he was paid to fight—*not* the battles of his heart.

That was not who he was anymore.

But he wasn't so sure. He was slipping.

"Only ten rials." An old woman's voice jerked him sharply back.

"What?"

"That oil you're holding, I'll give it to you for only ten rials."

Rafiq looked numbly down at the bottle of scented bath oil in his hand. When had he picked this up? What in hell was wrong with him?

He turned the bottle over slowly in palm. He used to buy gifts like this for Nahla. He looked up sharply. "I'll give you nine."

Crinkles fanned out around the woman's eyes. She took the oil from him, began to wrap it. "She will like it."

"Who will?"

"Your woman, yes?"

"She's not my—"

"You would like anything else, maybe some lotion, like this one?" She held out her hand, palm up, over a jar of almond butter.

"Ah, yeah, sure." Paige needed lotion. The desert was dry. This was not about buying gifts. He'd abducted her and she'd been able to bring nothing with her. "And I'll take that, and that, and that there." He pointed to a bottle of shampoo, then another vial of perfumed oil, a piece of silver ribbon and a hairbrush.

The woman took his handful of gold coins and handed

him his package. Rafiq felt a rush in his chest as he took the bundle of goods. And he had to convince himself that he had not drifted with the moment. That it was not about gratuitous presents for Paige, or about making amends for his actions.

This was about need.

He knew even a cool-headed scientist like Paige Sterling was not above wanting to feel desirable. And he wanted to make her feel that way.

He tucked the package under his arm and blew out a breath. Then he looked toward the stall where he'd left Paige.

She was coming around the table. He could tell it was her by the way she moved. He could hear the chink of bells as she approached.

"Hey," she said, a soft smile in her eyes. They were lined with black kohl that made them look hauntingly silver. Luminous. Just looking into them made him feel as if he'd been punched in the gut.

"What's in the package?" she asked.

"Ah…nothing," he said, his gaze falling to her feet. They were covered with an intricate pattern painted in rose-brown henna, and she was wearing thonged sandals. The bells that hung from the silver ankle chains he'd bought peeped out from under the hem of her *chador.*

She held out her hands for him to see, turned them over. They, too, had been expertly darkened with henna patterns, and her fingers were adorned in silver rings. Rafiq swallowed. He hadn't made this woman disappear— she'd been reinvented. And he wasn't quite sure what to do about it.

"Do you approve?" she asked in Arabic, her haunting eyes searching his.

"Ah…yes. She, um, she did an excellent job. You look like the real deal."

"And now?"

"Now what?"

"Where do we go from here?" she asked softly.

His pulse quickened and he felt his mouth go dry. *I really don't know where we go from here, Paige.* Then he snapped himself together. "We should head back to the apartment, see how the download is going. This new look should get you past the Land Command at the gates."

Her eyes flickered nervously.

"Come." He held out his hand, palm up, and she placed hers in his. He closed his hand around her fingers and looked once more into her eyes. And he just knew he was going to keep her safe—no matter the cost.

This time he'd get the woman out of Na'jif.

"You'll be fine," he said. "Just walk like you belong with me, okay?"

They moved out of the market area, through the stone archway at the north end. The group of soldiers stationed at the base of the ancient arch stopped laughing and fell silent. They turned their eyes on her.

Her legs suddenly felt wooden. Each time she took a step, the bells at her ankles chinked, making her even more self-conscious. She felt as if she may as well be wearing a banner on her back that blared *Imposter*! Her heart began to race again.

But Rafiq, sensing her unease, slipped his arm around her waist and moved her body closer to his. She took her cue from his steps, felt herself move in concert with him, drawing from his confidence.

They cleared the arch, and the men resumed talking.

Relief punched out of her, making her slightly giddy. But Rafiq did not let go of her waist, and she didn't move away, either. He felt good. She liked the way he touched her, the way he moved *with* her. She liked his smoldering self-assurance, and the way he made her feel safe, and feminine.

She'd never known a man like this.

Rafiq guided her to a busy intersection and they waited for the traffic to pass. Paige watched the carts, trucks, camels and bicycles through the slit in the fabric of her *chador,* her new window on the world. The garment restricted her peripheral vision even more than the helmet on her hazmat suit did, but she also felt protected from her enemies, and because of it, strangely free to relax and be herself inside.

She watched a group of women, floating spectral figures in black, approach the intersection on the opposite side of the road. They stepped off the curb and the traffic stopped. In awe, Paige watched them drift across the cobbled street and she heard the soft chorus of bells as they moved.

Men turned to look and the street sounds almost became hushed as people listened to the sound of the women walking. One of the women angled her head, said something, and the others laughed. Paige realized with a start that they were young, perhaps in their late teens, and clearly aware of the attention they'd attracted, enjoying it.

Even under all those black veils, these young women had found a way to look sexy and stop traffic. Their layers of hidden mystery and whispering fabric only served to pique sensual interest. She shook her head and smiled to herself.

She could only imagine the depth of a man's enjoyment at finally seeing a woman's naked thighs, her belly, the curve of her shoulders.

The thought of sex made her glance at Rafiq. She was shocked to realize he'd been watching her, his black eyes intense. She felt her cheeks flush, her body heat. She flicked her eyes away, relieved he couldn't see under her veil.

The traffic light changed, and Rafiq increased the pressure of his hand on the small of her back, escorting her proprietarily over the street. Paige couldn't help but notice men glance her way, and she wondered if she, too, looked as if she were floating.

Rafiq realized too late that he'd turned into *the* street. He hesitated.

Paige threw him a questioning glance. "Are we going the wrong way?"

No. It was the right way, just the wrong time. He stared down the twisting street with its ornate lampposts and wooden shuttered windows…and it took his mind back, drew him down over the worn cobblestones…toward her house.

He began to walk, his feet operating of their own volition, his heart a slow, steady thud against his chest. The world, the present, morphed into a blur around him. He was barely conscious of Paige at his side.

The shutters were still painted green. The iron lamppost still stood under her window.

Rafiq stopped.

In a distant part of his brain, he could feel the tension in Paige's body, feel her eyes on him. But he'd gone beyond it now. He was back.

And he couldn't tear himself away.

Fifteen years.

A decade and a half since Nahla had blown him her last kiss from that window, her hair burnished black in the gold light of that lamp. His throat burned. His vision blurred. And a wave of blinding rage slammed into his heart. His grip tightened on Paige's arm.

"Rafiq?" she whispered. Concern, he could hear it in her voice. His captive was showing concern for *him*. For his anguish. He didn't want her concern.

He wanted revenge.

"Rafiq!"

Her voice jerked him back. "What is it? What the hell's going on?" She spoke in Arabic, her voice low, urgent with an edge of fear.

But he couldn't answer. He couldn't talk at all. He stared at Nahla's house and the years unraveled in a string of memories. He could recall exactly how he felt that night he came back here, the night he'd returned from Paris. Eagerness had lightened his step and his heart, and he'd felt the ring burning a hole in the pocket of his robes.

But it wasn't Nahla who'd greeted him at that door. It was her brothers, grim and gray and bent with the news. It had sunk through him like a rock; he'd steadied himself with a hand on that doorjamb. He could feel it now, against his palm. And in his mind's eye he could see her mother, crumpled over the kitchen table in grief...and her father, pacing, worried about the shame brought on his family.

Paige's hand closed over his arm. "We should go, Rafiq. People are watching."

He blinked as the door of the house opened and an old woman stepped into the frame. She stared at him. His heart began to jackhammer, his skin turned hot. She wasn't just staring at him, she was looking right into him. *Could she know?* Could she see beneath his turban and cheap burlap robes?

Seconds, minutes ticked by. But he could not tear his eyes away from hers, an unspoken communication stretching tautly and vibrating across the stretch of street between them.

Then the old woman slowly lifted her veil, exposing her face, her eyes to him, showing him exactly who she was. Even from here, he could see the wrinkles cleft by years of pain and sadness. The string of memories tightened around his neck like a noose. He couldn't breathe.

"Rafiq!" Paige shook his arm, trying to pull him out of the death grip of the past. "Rafiq! I don't know what's going on with you, but I'm getting the hell out of here before you attract the attention of the police."

She jerked away, her movement yanking him back. And with a jolt, he realized he'd completely lost it. He glanced once more at the old woman, but she was gone, dematerialized like a sepulchral figment of his past.

Had he even seen her? Panic kicked at him.

This had been a terrible mistake. They had to lie low until they could get out of town. Because if she'd recognized him, and he was sure she had, the mission would be scuttled. The whole bloody country would blow.

The Cabal would unleash the plague.

He swore viciously under his breath, turned on his heels and ran down the street, Paige in his wake, her black robes flying out behind her.

* * *

19:02 Charlie, Nexus Compound, Thursday, October 2

The man stood on the edge of the cliff, hot wind flapping his robes about his ankles, the tail of his turban flaying against his shoulder. His eyes narrowed into the bite of salt off the sea.

He'd already seen the puddle of brake fluid, the vehicle tracks. Most of it had been made by emergency personnel, but he was a tracker, a hunter, and he could read what few could see. And he'd seen something—footprints that had been brushed over with deft and hurried flicks of a hand, tracks through flinty ground, a patch of uneven sand under the compound fence.

He lifted his chin, nostrils flaring to the wind. Then he spun abruptly on his heels.

He had work to do.

Chapter 7

Paige reached for a falafel, dipped it in cucumber sauce and took a bite. She chewed, watching him work at the desk, tension rolling off him in waves.

She'd bet her last dollar that he didn't have to be fiddling with that equipment right now. It was a displacement activity, his way of avoiding whatever it was that had come back to haunt him in the streets of Na'jif.

Rafiq Zayed may be an FDS merc, but he definitely had ties to this place. He had a serious history here.

She took another bite, chewed on both the food and the mystery. She knew she would not be able to let it rest until she unearthed his story, or discovered who that old woman in the doorway was. Lifting a veil to a man like that was blasphemous and literally criminal in this culture. That woman knew him. And he knew her. Paige was certain of it.

She reached for another falafel. "This food is good," she called out to him. "And it's going to be all gone soon if you don't come and help me eat."

He didn't turn around.

"You not hungry?"

He lifted his head, loose hair gleaming on his shoulders under the light of the lamp. He sat like that for a second, his back to her, as if composing himself. Then he stood, came over, lowered himself to the cushions beside her, and reached for a flatbread.

He ate in silence.

A muezzin chanted, his haunting call to night prayers ricocheting through the city alleys and bouncing off minarets. A thin sickle moon was rising over the distant Asir Mountains, and stars were beginning to dot the darkening sky. Beyond the city walls, the vast silence of the desert seemed to creep in and hush the day.

Paige watched Rafiq chew. His mouth was beautiful, sculpted, and his luminous eyes were seeing something a million miles away. She touched his arm. "Rafiq?"

He tensed and his eyes flashed to hers, suddenly hot, glittering. The man was like a beast caged in his own body.

"Why Na'jif?" she asked.

His brows shot up in question.

"I mean, there *are* other places you could've gone to do the download."

He slowly finished his mouthful. "Na'jif is within range of the transmitting device." Then, realizing he hadn't answered her question, he said, "And it was an ideal place to find a safe house. The roots of the underground network go deep here. The heart of the rebellion lies in Na'jif."

This she had not known.

"Besides," he added, reaching for the jug of mint tea and pouring two glasses, one first for her and one for himself, "I am familiar with the place."

That was obvious after today, in the way he'd moved seamlessly through the market, the warren of city streets, in the way he'd looked at that woman, that house.

"Why is Na'jif the heart of the rebellion?" she asked, careful not to push too hard, or too fast.

He took a long sip of tea and sat silent for a while. The faint sound of music and laughter drifted over the rooftops.

"Something happened here once," he said abruptly, his voice holding no room for further questions or argument.

"What happened?" she asked softly.

He got to his feet in a liquid motion. "Eat. I have work to do."

02:37 Charlie, Na'jif safe house, Friday, October, 3

Rafiq stared at the screen, the glow from his monitor providing the only light in the apartment as the hours ticked down to dawn. The tech crew in São Diogo was making good progress. Information was being relayed from the Nexus system much faster than anticipated.

The crew was decoding the data as it came in and passing it on to Dr. Jan Meyer and the biotech team they had assembled. Meyer was a world-renowned infectious disease specialist affiliated with the Leopold Institute in Belgium and a consultant for a consortium of European Union intelligence. The FDS had brought him in to interpret the medical data. It had been Meyer who had alerted them to Nexus and Paige Sterling's specific field of interest in the first place, after he'd identified the pathogen they'd brought out of the Congo jungle.

Anticipation rustled through Rafiq as he watched the stream of data flick faster over his screen. If this kept up, they could be out of here by tomorrow night. And not a moment too soon.

He glanced over at Paige, who had fallen asleep, out under the open sky on a Persian rug and pillows. Her pale hair fanned about her face, gleaming in the moonlight. A tenderness he could not begin to explain filled his heart, and the heat of desire swelled deep in him. She stirred, as if she could sense him looking, lifted her head sleepily, then jerked upright in shock as she realized where she was.

"Hey," he said.

"Hey to you, too." Her voice was husky from sleep, her eyes dreamy. She pushed her hair back from her forehead. He couldn't help but watch her mouth. All he could think of was how kissable it looked right now. He felt himself grow hard.

"What time is it?"

He cleared his throat. "Going on 3 a.m."

"Good Lord, I hadn't meant to fall asleep there." She pushed herself stiffly to her feet, her black skirt crumpled from sleep, her blouse open provocatively. He swallowed, his eyes fixed on her breasts.

She pulled her blouse over her chest as she hobbled toward him. "I could do with a bath. Is there any hot water in there?" She gestured to the living quarters and bathroom.

"As much as you like," he said, watching her limp. "Your leg okay?"

Something flitted over her features, a memory of her abduction, perhaps, and then it was gone. "It's fine, just a cut and bruise that's gotten a bit swollen."

"I'm sorry."

She held his gaze. "It's for a greater cause, and all that. Right?"

"Right."

Her mouth flattened and she continued to the door and disappeared around the trellis, making her way into the apartment.

He stared after her, conscious of the heat in his groin, his heavy breathing. She was upset because he hadn't answered her questions, because he'd cut her off. He couldn't blame her. He couldn't tell her, either.

No one could know he was back.

"I'll get you some ointment," he called after her, but he wasn't sure if she'd heard him. "I'll leave it outside the bathroom door," he muttered to himself, turning back to his computer. But he couldn't concentrate.

He hadn't told *anyone* about his past, not even his FDS colleagues. He'd reached a point where he'd barely even acknowledged it to himself anymore. But now, after all these years of being comfortably numb, this mission had forced him to come full circle, back to the very heart of Na'jif, and the feelings that he was having to confront again were overwhelming. Paige wasn't helping, either.

How much longer could he be with her, without touching her—intimately?

And if he did, could he ever go back to the way he was? Perhaps he'd already crossed that line...when he'd gathered her into his arms and held her while she cried, when he'd walked with her in the market, holding her hand as if she belonged to him, when he'd bought her those gifts.

He somehow doubted he'd ever be able to shield his heart in the same way again once he left Hamān this time. A man did that kind of thing only once in his life. And a little niggling part of him wondered if he really wanted to be numb again.

His mind drifted back to that night in the tiny Parisian bar, to the first drink of alcohol he'd ever had in his life. He'd been desperate to drown his agony and annihilate his ties to his heritage with the same bottle.

Many drinks later, a man had come in—a tall dark stranger with a look of murder in his ice-gray eyes and a fearsome scar down the side of his face. That man had recognized something in Rafiq, a kinship. The man had sat down across from him, bought him another bottle, poured himself a drink, and they'd gotten drunk together. He'd told Rafiq he knew how a man could bury his past, completely. He was going to do it himself. And *if* he survived the next five years, he'd come out with an official new identity—a new name and a French passport.

That man was Jacques Sauvage.

And the next day Rafiq had found himself with Sauvage in front of the gates of the French Foreign Legion in Fort de Nogent, Paris. When those gates had clanged shut behind them, the men they'd once been had ceased to exist.

Rafiq never asked Jacques about the scar, and no one ever asked Rafiq about his own past.

It had been the right thing at the time, the *only* thing that had kept him living. And fighting. So why was he *feeling* again, why now? Why could he not *keep* those damn gates shut?

He jerked sharply to his feet, dragged both hands through his hair. Questions were a waste of time. He had to focus on completing this mission. Millions of lives depended on it.

He stalked over to the edge of the parapet, as restless as a caged tiger. And just as hungry…for something he couldn't have, and shouldn't even want.

Paige sighed deeply as she sank down into the hot and fragrant water, letting it lap right up against her chin.

The ceramic tub had clawed feet that looked like the talons of a griffin and it was positioned in front of a long window. She'd thrown the shutters open, and the candles she'd lit flickered in the soft, warm air. Paige rested her head back and watched the sky, searching for constellations she could recognize. Slowly, her body began to relax.

As frustrated as she was with Rafiq for brushing her off like that, she was touched with the package she'd discovered in the bathroom. He'd actually bought her cosmetics at the market. No one had bought her cosmetics before. Ever. No one had even thought she'd ever want a gift like that. How could she blame them? She'd grown up in jungles, far away from malls, from girlfriends, movies, magazines. And when she'd been forced to move back into mainstream society, all alone at the age of fifteen, she had never showed the side of herself that wanted pretty things, in part in deference to her parents' memories. They'd always eschewed that kind of thing. But somehow, Rafiq had picked up on her secret need. She sank deeper into the tub.

Maybe he'd just done it out of some guilt trip. The man was an enigma. And after today, she could see that there was some real deep, dark stuff swirling around in his psyche. Even if his silence irked her, the knowledge that he was vulnerable under all that brawn and bravado somehow endeared him to her.

And made her desperately curious.

"Curiosity killed the cat, Paige," she reminded herself as she dipped right under the water.

It was almost dawn by the time Paige had dried off. She peered into an ornate oval mirror hanging above a black marble basin and barely recognized the face that stared back.

The skin around her eyes—usually pale and drawn from hours in the lab—was still dark from kohl, giving her a mysterious look. She lifted her hand to push her damp hair back from her face and the glimmer of silver rings and bracelets caught the candlelight. A ghost of a smile touched her lips. The scientist who never wore jewelry was adorned with the stuff. It wasn't that she didn't like it, it just wasn't practical—or safe. She worked in a space suit where a tiny puncture could spell death. And she had daily chemical showers and little time to think of dressing up, let alone attracting the opposite sex.

But somehow, in stealing her away from the compound, Rafiq had temporarily stolen her away from that aspect of her life. And now there was a new quality in her eyes. A wildness, a playfulness. And it hit her—she'd been both captured and set free at the same time.

She did not want to even begin to analyze that.

A knock on the door startled her.

Paige quickly twisted a towel over her head, grabbed another and wrapped it around her, opened the door a crack and peered out.

There was no one there, just a dark-blue apothecary jar and a box of plasters—both with Arabic lettering—left on the hall table beside the bathroom door. Under them was a neatly folded garment of sheer white silk.

Paige looked up and down the passageway, but there was no sign of anyone.

She gathered up the items and closed the bathroom door behind her. Obviously Rafiq had left her disinfectant, bandages if she needed them, and a change of clothes. She shook the garment out and a note fell from the folds.

She picked it up, read it. It said she should leave her clothes in a pile at the door, and that they would be washed and dried. In the meantime, she must wear the caftan. He apologized for it being too big, but it was the only appropriate thing he could find in the apartment owner's closet.

Paige smiled, pressed the note to her lips, and realized she had totally lost it. The most disturbing thing about this self-revelation was, she didn't actually care.

The bells around her ankles chinked softly as she made her way back to the patio. The silk caftan whispered over her skin, softened with almond lotion, and Paige felt like a completely new woman.

4:19 Charlie, Nexus compound, Friday, October 3

The man stepped into Dr. Sterling's office. He didn't flick on the lights, not at first. He just stood still, fingers twitching at his side, sensing the environment in the dull orange glow of night-lights.

Chimps shrieked down the hall. The air smelled like chemicals. It had been like this when she'd last clocked out. She'd been working later than usual. Why?

He swiveled sharply on his heels, stared at her computer.

He needed to get a look in there.

He flipped the light switch and neon flickered starkly.

Then light burst through the room, throwing his reflection onto the glass that looked into her dark lab.

He dropped to his haunches, studied the floor. A small dark spot caught his eye. He licked his finger, rubbed it into the spot, put it against the tip of his tongue.

Blood.

He closed his eyes in controlled pleasure. He had the scent.

Of death.

5:07 Charlie, Na'jif safe house, Friday, October 3

He heard the soft pulse of bells. Rafiq sat up, rubbed his eyes. It was almost dawn, he must have dozed off in front of his computer. But the sound of bells was not a dream. It was Paige. He could sense her behind him. And he could smell the fragrance he'd bought for her.

He inhaled slowly, turned in his chair, looked up— and swallowed.

She was wearing the caftan. Beneath that silk Paige was naked, apart from the chains he'd bought for her ankles, the bangles around her wrists and the silver rings that adorned her fingers. Her hair lay tousled and damp on her shoulders.

Pleasure rippled through Rafiq.

He raked his eyes brazenly over her body, stopping where her breasts rose firmly under the opalescent fabric. Then he lifted his eyes, met hers.

She held his gaze steadily, and he could see the light in her eyes was different.

His pulse quickened, the sensation pleasant, like the rush from caffeine. He moistened his lips.

If it were another woman, he'd take her now, right there on that Persian rug. But she was the mastermind behind the bioweapon that threatened the future of democracy. She was his mission.

And she had a damn unsettling way of blurring the boundaries.

Rafiq swallowed, suddenly unsure of himself.

"Thank you," she said in Arabic, her voice soft, her pronunciation perfect.

"For what?" His voice was thick.

"The clothes, the ointment, the oils." She smiled and the reflected light from his monitor sparkled in her eyes. "And the hairbrush."

He must be dreaming. That couldn't really be the smoky tone of seduction in her voice. He couldn't really see the dusky shape of her nipples under the caftan. They weren't really pressed erect against the sheer embroidered fabric. She wasn't really turned on by him.

He wasn't hot at all.

Her ran his hand over his hair, trying to focus. "It's nothing," he said. "It's…my pleasure." She didn't know the half of it. "It was the least I could do."

She looked away, her damp hair hiding her profile. Guilt twinged through him.

He stood, took her hand in his. It was soft and warm from her bath. "Paige?"

She turned her head to face him. Her eyes were luminous, her lips parted. Blood rushed instantly from his head and he felt light. He drew her closer. "Paige, I—" A loud beeping sounded from his computer.

He spun round, leaned over the desk, hit a key. A countdown clock flashed onto the screen, and his adrenaline spiked. *Yes!* In eleven hours, five minutes and fifty-three seconds, the download would be complete and the mission accomplished. They'd be out of here by nightfall.

He hit another key and realized Paige was right beside him, sharing his energy, bending over the desk, trying to see the monitor, the swell of her breast brushing against his arm.

He stilled.

His heart began to thud. Hard.

He turned his face slowly to her, and for a moment he couldn't breathe. The way she was leaning over his desk he could see right down her caftan. Heat swamped his belly, and his mind went blank.

He leaned forward, pressing his arm more firmly against her breast, his mouth moving closer to hers.

She didn't pull away.

Her lips parted for him. She leaned forward. His vision swam, and he brushed his lips ever so lightly over hers—a caress, a question.

She answered, moving her lips against his, a soft whisper of pleasure escaping her throat.

His stomach swooped violently. He raised his hand, cupped the back of her neck, pulled her into him…as static crackled sharply. "Zayed, you there?"

They both jerked back, shocked at what had just happened. For a second, they just stared at each other, their attraction—rich and carnal—surging between them.

Rafiq shook himself.

He leaned over, tweaked a dial on his equipment. "*Oui,* I'm here." His voice was thick, even to his own ears.

"You were sleeping, *mon ami.*" He heard the laugh in his colleague's voice.

"*Non.*" Not with her. Not yet.

"*Ça va.* Progress is good. Very good. We have access to

all Nexus quadrants, but as far as the data analysis goes, things would go even faster if we had the passwords, to Dr. Sterling's system in particular. There's some heavy encryption. If you can get the codes from her, it will save days. Maybe lives."

"Affirmative." He glanced at Paige. She'd heard everything.

And suddenly she looked terrified. She took a step back, folded her arms over her stomach. Her body language was unmistakable. She was shutting down.

"Paige—"

"Get me out of Hamān first. Then I'll give you *everything* you want."

"Paige, you heard him." Rafiq pointed to his computer. "Getting those codes early could save lives."

She shook her head, her eyes narrowing. "Rafiq, please. Get me out of Hamān, and then I will help with everything I can."

He cursed, dragged his hands over his hair. "You don't trust me, is that what this is about?"

She hesitated.

"Look, I *will* get you out, I promise." But he could see the doubt in her eyes.

"You tell me you're a soldier with the FDS, Rafiq. Yet you clearly have some history right here in Hamān. For all I know, you really could be some member of the Silent Revolution. What guarantee do I have that you're not going to finish that download, get what you need from me, and then leave me here?"

Frustration nipped at him. "Oh, come on, Paige. If I wanted to get rid of you, I would have done it already."

Her mouth went flat.

He blew out air in irritation "I thought you understood the scope of this. I thought you said you were innocent, that you wanted to help. Was that a lie?"

She took another step back, her jaw lifting in defiance. "I mean it, Rafiq."

He felt himself tense. "Dammit, Paige, I told you what's at stake here. If you don't give us those codes—"

"Then what?"

"Then we hack in anyway, and Dr. Meyer and his team will get to work. All you do is cost us time—time it takes to save lives."

She blinked sharply. *"Jan Meyer?"*

"You know him?"

She went deathly pale. "I…he…my father…" She cleared her throat. "My father went to see Dr. Meyer in Brussels, just before my parents disappeared in the Congo. I was fifteen. I remember it well because my mother and father…they had a really big argument about it when he came back." She swallowed, sat slowly on the chaise lounge where he'd tossed his tunic.

"They never used to fight like that. They went into the jungle together, angry with each other. I…never saw them again. They never came back."

He took a step toward her, his interest piqued. "Do you know why your father went to see Meyer?"

She shook her head.

"I do."

Her eyes flared wide. "What!"

"Meyer told us that your father went to Brussels to talk to him about the disease he'd discovered in the Blacklands bonobos. He wanted to meet Meyer in secret because he was contracted not to discuss his research, yet he felt the information was vital to the scientific community. He said it defied all current scientific thinking about prion diseases. But," he said, "your father never showed up for their meeting the next day. He went back to the Congo."

She went sheet-pale.

"Meyer thinks he either chickened out, or someone got to him."

"What do you mean, 'got to him'?"

He took another step toward her. "Your parents were being funded by Science Reach International at the time, the same company that funded *your* pet project, Paige. The same project *you* picked up from your father and mother. And don't tell me you didn't know that Science Reach is indirectly controlled by Nexus, and in turn by BioMed." He paused, watching her eyes carefully. "Your father's need to share with the international scientific community probably killed your parents."

She swayed slightly. "*What* did you say?"

He hated doing this, but if she really didn't know it, she needed to. "You heard me. These guys you work for don't mess around. Now give me those codes, Paige, and we can stop them from hurting more people."

She sat open-mouthed, staring at him, disbelief in her eyes.

"It was Meyer who helped us identify the pathogen, Paige. He pointed us to Nexus, to you—precisely because of that incident with your father all those years ago, and because he knew you had picked up your parents' research."

Nausea rode up through her stomach. Her heart began to palpitate. Her hands felt sweaty. Science Reach International *had* actively recruited her right after she'd shown interest in obtaining her father's work. They'd funded all her university studies, paid for her apartment, meals, books. And then Nexus had hired her to do research that could ultimately be marketed by BioMed. She could not even begin to digest the scope of what Rafiq had just said. It…would mean her entire life had been a farce—that she'd been manipulated since she was a child. That she and her parents had been *owned* by a corporation.

Had her mother and father really been *murdered?*

Had her mom and dad been trying to get out? Was that what the big fight had been about, the night before they vanished?

She sniffed back the emotion threatening her eyes, and fear burned in her gut. She had to hold on to what little control she had left. Information was her *only* tradeable commodity right now. It was the only thing she had left to fight back at the world with.

She looked up at Rafiq. "I will not give you my pass codes until you get me out of Hamān," she said, clearly, crisply.

"Paige—"

She pulled her shoulders back. "You heard me."

He took another step toward her and she braced.

"We have only ten days until—"

"I have no reason to believe you, Rafiq. You won't tell me anything about yourself. You owe me nothing. Why should I be so naive as to think you'll get me out of the country because you *promised?*"

He went rigid. Fire crackled in his eyes, and the muscles of his neck bunched tight. "Paige," he growled.

She tilted her chin.

He stepped right up to her, his fists clenching at his sides.

Her heart began to pound wildly, but she held herself steady.

"I'll give you two hours to collect your thoughts, Dr. Sterling." His eyes skewered hers. "If you're not going to help us, we have no need of you." He held two fingers up in front of her face. "Two hours. That's it." He let the warning hang between them. "And if you don't talk, I leave Na'jif without you."

She glowered back at him but fear clawed at her insides. He was bluffing. Had to be.

He walked back to the desk, stopped, turned round. "And in ten days, after D-day, *if* you're still alive, *if* you've survived the brutality of the Land Command, the FDS will send the might of the American military after you."

He gave her a slow, measured look. "Do you know what that means? Do you know what the new laws will do to a terrorist like you? You have committed treason, Paige."

"I have not. I've been used."

"Perhaps," he said coldly. "But right at this minute, you have the ability to act fast and in doing so maybe save millions of innocent lives. But you choose not to, even knowing the consequences. How do you think that is going to go down in the States when word gets out? How do you think they will handle you when they find out *you* engineered the pathogen that's killing President Elliot, one of the most beloved U.S. leaders in recent history? You're going to be considered a murderer, Paige. An assassin."

She swallowed.

Her throat burned, her eyes blurred. "I *will* help. I'll do everything I possibly can." Her voice had gone small. "Just please get me out of Hamān first, to a place where I am free to contact a U.S. embassy and find out if you are legitimate…and where I can find a lawyer."

He held up his fingers. "Two hours."

Paige locked herself in the bathroom, slumped onto the laundry basket and clutched the key she'd taken from the pocket of his tunic. She was numb. Confused. Frightened.

Rafiq was putting the screws to her because her codes were obviously of vital importance to him—but he'd just shattered her identity, her purpose in life.

Paige rocked back and forth on the basket, a blanket of despair settling cold and heavy over her shoulders. She tried to think it through—her parents' research project in the Congo, the Science Reach funding, the argument over visiting Meyer. Her parents must have been afraid. She supposed it was feasible they had been killed because of what they knew. People were killed for lesser secrets. What her father had found had been earth-shattering. It went against the grain of all current scientific thinking on how prion illnesses were caused, and because of this, Paige had been able to isolate potential antidotes. This represented a fortune in technology and medicines.

But *who* had done this to them? What person had ordered them dead?

And what would they do if they knew she was still alive?

She looked up, her eyes sore and dry. The sun was rising behind the mountains. She stood, went to the window. Beyond those purple ridges in the distance lay the Empty Quarter, a barren wasteland.

Like her soul.

Paige leaned out the window and peered down. There

was a ridge, just a few inches wide, that ran along the wall under the window.

What did she have to lose? A life in prison? Humiliation. Degradation. What would her parents do?

She looked back up at the mountains, fingering the key in her hand. Freedom. There was freedom in death, wasn't there? Because the chances she'd make it to those mountains and beyond was close to nil.

It wasn't in her to take her own life. She didn't have the courage to do that. But she was prepared to die fighting for survival.

But *if* she made it to those mountains, she could cross the border into Saudi Arabia. Maybe she could forget her name, who she was, what she'd done...maybe she could just disappear into the fabric of the desert.

She was dead to the world anyway.

She really did have nothing to lose.

Chapter 8

Rafiq drummed his fingers on the desk. It had been more than two hours and she still hadn't come out of the bathroom.

He jerked to his feet, stormed into the living quarters, raised his fist and banged on the door. "Paige! Time's up."

Silence. Unease skittered through him.

"Paige! You're trying my patience!"

Nothing.

"Paige?" He tried the brass handle. The door was locked. *Damn.* He braced himself and kicked the door. It splintered open and banged back with a crash.

The bathroom was empty, a shutter swinging loosely in the breeze. His heart kicked against his chest. *What the hell?*

He lunged for the window, leaned out, peered down,

saw the crumbling parapet. She could not possibly have worked her way along that. She had to be somewhere in the apartment.

He swiveled round, saw the folded piece of paper on the floor. He bent down, grabbed it, opened it. There were six lines written across the page consisting of a mix of letters and numerals, followed by a set of instructions.

The pass codes.

His eyes shot to the window and a hollowness filled his chest. Could she actually have gotten out there? No. They were three floors up. Maybe she just wanted him to believe she had. She could be hiding, waiting for an opportunity to slip out behind his back.

He stormed out of the bathroom and down the tiled corridor, a wedge of disquiet driving into his chest. "Paige!"

He got to the main bedroom and his heart stalled. The doors to the owner's armoire hung open. A pile of clothing and scarves was scattered over the floor, as if she'd flung them out as she rummaged through them. He crouched down, touched the clothes. *Men's* clothes.

He lurched to his feet, stormed down the passage, yanked on the front door handle. It opened. *It was unlocked.* A sick sensation filled his gut.

He dashed to the chaise lounge, checked his tunic pocket. The key was gone.

He swore violently. How could he have been so stupid, so trusting? It was the damn woman. She was messing with his brain and his libido.

He jerked his head up, marshalling his thoughts. She'd disguised herself as a man. She was going to try and escape Na'jif, make a run for it.

Rafiq spun round, faced the parapet. He looked out over

the city, tension bunching the muscles in his neck. The dawn sun was bursting over the mountains and hitting the tall turrets and the gold dome of the mosque.

A muezzin began to chant. *Dawn prayers.* Every man who valued his life would be moving off the streets and into a designated place of worship at this very minute. If there were Land Command soldiers out there, if they saw her, dressed like a man…*she'd never make it.*

If they captured her, discovered she was a woman under those clothes…Rafiq clenched his jaw. He spun on his heels, grabbed his tunic, flung his turban over his head, shoved his *jambiya* into his belt, and dashed down the narrow whitewashed steps three at a time.

He charged into the stable area yelling for a horse.

Stable hands still too young to be ordered to prayers scrambled barefoot in his wake. Rafiq grabbed one by the scruff of his tunic. "Did anyone come through here in the last hour? A young man?"

The boy's eyes went huge with fear.

Rafiq tightened his grip. "Speak, boy! You see *anyone?*"

The boy's cheeks went red and he nodded.

"Which way did sh…*he* go?"

"He…he took a horse, sir. I…I unlocked the gate for him and let him out."

Rafiq's eyes shot to the narrow covered alley that led down to the wrought iron gate. "Did you see which way he rode?"

"To…to the city gates, sir. We ran after him for a while."

He dropped the boy. "Open that gate, now!" The kid scurried down the narrow alley. Rafiq grabbed the reins of an already saddled stallion out the hands of another lad, swung himself into the saddle and kicked his mount into action.

His head was down and he was at a full gallop by the time he reached the end of the narrow corridor. He charged straight at the wrought iron-gate where the child fumbled the key with panicked hands.

"Hurry!" he screamed in Arabic, showing no intention of slowing for what barred his way.

The kid flung the gate open with a split second to spare. It clanged back against the whitewashed wall, chips of plaster flying.

Rafiq barreled out into the street, his stallion's hooves clattering over cobblestones. Chickens scattered out from under him in a squawking blizzard of white and brown feathers, and a goat bleated as it scampered for shelter. A woman screamed at him, waving her broom.

He broke out of the narrow and shadowed road into a wide main street which was lit with the gold light of dawn. It was eerily quiet at this precise hour, the prayer hour. The only people moving along the sidewalks were women, who stopped dead and stared as he thundered past.

He rode, his heart thudding with the rhythm of the hooves, knowing that each second he was out here he was risking an informant snitching on him, risking the wrath of the sultan's Land Command, risking his life. But *nothing* in the world could have kept him from going after Paige. Never again would he allow Sadiq or his men to hurt a woman—especially one who was supposed to be in his care.

He would die first. After he'd killed the bastard himself.

He slapped at the horse and he cursed himself for having spoken to her so harshly, for causing her to flee. He'd only wanted to shake her into releasing the information. Sauvage had been clear—*do what it takes.*

Now he had that information, and he'd lost her.

And instead of immediately relaying the codes to Sauvage, he'd pursued her, knowing he might never come back. He could not have done otherwise. He'd acted on gut response. It was the way Rafiq had always lived—before he'd fled Hamān, and learned not to feel.

But those barriers were broken now. He was back. And so was the full force of his fire.

He reached the city gates, churned through them like a bat out of hell and thundered into the desert in a cloud of sand. He jerked the reins and his stallion reared to a stop.

Rafiq scanned the rolling sands. There she was, a small plume of dust rising in the distance. It had to be her—making a beeline for the Asir—the only fool riding beyond the city walls at prayer hour.

"Yaah!" he yelled, kicking at his horse. He charged into the sands, aiming for that faint cloud of dust blowing like spindrift in the wind.

He began to close in on her, coming at her from an angle. She was still a speck in a rippled wasteland, and she rode as if she'd been born on a horse, bent low, robes flying out behind her.

She looked backward, then kicked her horse faster, veered to the right. The woman had a death wish. What could he expect? She was a woman without options. *He'd* done that to her.

"Yaaah!" He yelled again and urged the stallion to move even faster, hooves thudding hollow on the sand, dust boiling out behind him.

He closed the gap, came up behind her, rode harder until he was level with her mount.

His horse was panting hard. His heart thudded in his chest. He leaned over, reached for her bridle, missed as she swerved sharply sideways. He caught himself. Hot damn, she was good.

He swung his horse after her hers, galloped harder, both beasts snorting heavily now, heads nodding in unison as they raced side by side, spurred by each other. Sweat glistening. Dust sticking.

"Stop, Paige!" he yelled.

She kicked, rode even faster, robes flapping, turban flying loose from her hair. It streamed behind her, a pale gold beacon for the enemy to find.

Damn. He had to end this now!

He reined his horse, pulling the animal tight up against hers, adrenaline peaking in him, blood pounding through his veins. He hadn't ridden like this since that night he'd ridden from Na'jif. The night he'd gone to the palace to find Sadiq with murder in his heart.

He lunged for her saddle horn and swung himself onto the horse behind her, his stallion veering sharply away, still racing, riderless, a few yards to the side.

Rafiq tried to reach round her to grab the reins and wrest control of the horse from her grip. But she jerked her elbow back into his ribs, punching air out of him, almost knocking him off the left flank of the horse.

He struggled to correct his balance as she swung the animal to the right, trying to dislodge him further, but her horse stumbled under the suddenness of the movement throwing them both from the saddle.

Rafiq grabbed her as they went down. They hit the sand with a thud, breath exploding from his chest as he bore the brunt of their fall. They rolled fast and hard in the dirt. He kept his arms wrapped tight around her as they tumbled to a stop in a tangle of cloth and sand.

She squirmed instantly, trying to break his grip and scramble to her knees, but he wrestled her back to the ground and covered her body with his, holding her down.

And finally she stilled, her face pushed sideways into the sand. She was panting hard, damp with perspiration, her heart thudding. He could feel it beat against his chest.

"What in hell do you think you're doing!" He was breathing hard, too. He was furious. Memories of what Sadiq had done to Nahla swirled black and red and dangerous in his brain. The energy of it consumed him, powering a fierce and desperate need to protect through his blood.

"You want to get yourself killed, dammit! Do you know what they will do to you if they find you like this!"

She said nothing.

"You gonna stay put if I let you go?"

She made a small sound. He eased off her and she instantly squirmed out from under him and took off in a flat run. He lurched to his feet, dived and tackled her. They hit the ground hard. She spun her head around, bit him on the hand, breaking skin, drawing blood.

He cursed and covered her again with the full weight of his body. She flattened out onto the sand under him, suddenly limp, spent. So was he. He leaned heavily onto her, trying to catch his breath, his nose and mouth against her soft tangle of hair.

He lifted his head slowly, scanned the desert. He could see no telltale plume of sand. No one had come after them. Relief ebbed through him. He sat back. She pushed herself up into a sitting position, and turned to face him.

Her eyes were wild, glittering. Her hair was a tangled

halo full of sand, her cheek red from where he'd pushed it against coarse grains and her chin was grazed. She was still breathing hard.

His heart squeezed and a ball of emotion lodged in his throat. "Damn, Paige."

A shudder ran through her body and moisture filled her eyes. As he watched, one fat tear slipped down through the dust on her face.

He reached out, pulled her to him, held her gently against his chest, nestled his face in her hair. "Oh God, Paige, do you know what Sadiq does to the women who defy him? Do you understand how he hurts—*kills*—the people you love?"

She went still in his arms, listening.

"I won't let him do it again. Ever. To anyone." And the implications of what he'd just said hit him smack between the eyes. Because the only way to ensure Sadiq never hurt anyone ever again was to change the system. To get rid of him. To wrest control back from the evil that governed his country. Yes, *his* country!

This mission—this woman—had forced his hand. He knew what he had to do now. But first, he had to get Paige to safety.

She lifted her head, slowly raised her eyes to his. He could see the question in them.

He reached up, brushed sand off her cheek. "Why did you run, Paige?"

She wiped the back of her hand over her mouth, and he saw that it was shaking.

He took her hands in his. "Do you want to die? Because there's no way you'll make it out here. Not on your own."

"I'm dead to the world anyway. I…can't go back to the States. I have nothing left."

He looked right into those clear silver-gray eyes. "But you left me the codes. You decided to trust me."

"It's all I had left to give. My trust."

He closed his eyes for a second as feeling swam through him. She had no idea what her trust meant to him.

"I'm pathetic, Rafiq. A stupid fool for not seeing that I've been used all these years. I honestly never did anything with malicious intent." She took a deep, shuddering breath. "You'll find what you're looking for in Quadrant 3. I think that's the bioweapons arm of Nexus. I…I discovered something, just before you kidnapped me. I stole a vial that had been shipped in from the Congo. It had human brain tissue, infected with my pathogen." She sniffed, wiped her nose. "I…I didn't know what I was looking at, couldn't understand it, until now."

He studied her eyes. And he believed her implicitly. She'd been used. Just like Nahla had been used. But this time he was going to get her home safe. He was going to do everything in his power to see that she walked free.

A dry sob shuddered suddenly through her body. "Oh, Paige." He held her close, stroked her hair. "It's okay. We're going to get you through this. *I'm* going to get you through this. We're going to stop these guys."

She pulled back, sniffed again, wiped her sleeve over her nose. "Did…did you give your men the codes? Did they get into my computer?"

"*We* will give them the codes when we get back. Come." He held out his hand.

Her eyes opened wide. "You mean you came after me *first?*"

He didn't want to think about what that meant. "We must go, now. If your disguise holds, we might make it back into the city unnoticed."

She just stared at him.

He took her face in his hands, brushed his lips lightly over hers before he could even think about what he was doing. "Hang in there, okay?"

Incredulity crossed her features, her eyes opened even wider. She nodded, a small movement, and tears once again began to flow over her cheeks.

"Come now, let's find your turban and get you home."

But as he turned to go, she placed her hand on his arm. He stilled.

"Who did Sadiq hurt, Rafiq? Who was she?"

Rafiq gritted his teeth.

"Did you love her?" she whispered.

He flinched. Her eyes were so honest, open and caring. She'd been stripped down to nothing, and he needed to give her some measure of the truth if he wanted to keep her trust. He could see that now. She'd already seen right through him. She knew he had history in Na'jif.

"Yes. I loved her."

"So you *are* from Hamān."

"I *was* Hamānian. Once."

"What happened to her, Rafiq? Does it have something to do with that woman you saw yesterday?"

His chest went tight. He'd gone as far as he could. "That was her mother. But I did not come back for the past, Paige. I came only for the antidote. FDS sent me because I fit the local profile, and I speak the language. And that's the truth."

"But you didn't *want* to come back?"

"No," he said brusquely. "I wanted nothing more to do with this country."

"You're not going to tell me what happened here, are you?"

He sucked in his breath, blew it out sharply. "Let's just say there are a lot of reasons to leave this country."

"*And* to stay."

He frowned. "What do you mean?"

"This country needs people like you. The more there are, the greater the chances for a successful revolution, because it's going to happen. You know that."

He studied her features. "You really mean that, don't you? You really do care about these people."

"I do."

He nodded his head slowly. What kind of man did that make him? How could he have been gone like this for all these years? How could he have stopped caring?

He shook himself. He knew why. And he couldn't change that. What was done was done. But he was going to make damn sure he set things right now.

"Come," he said softly. "It's time to move. We've got a long ride ahead."

They rode back to Na'jif side by side, a team this time, linked by a tenuous bond and fragile understanding, a common mission and a rough road ahead of them.

10:38 Charlie, Nexus Lab Compound, Friday, October 3

He'd had a team of forensic techs working for more than five hours on the Nexus system. They'd started with her computer, and because they were looking so carefully, they'd seen something they might not have otherwise noticed—a whisper of an electronic trail that threaded into the heart of an entire system. They were working round the clock now to find out what it meant, and where it had been initiated.

He paced the corridor, impatient, edgy. Dr. Paige

Sterling hadn't been killed—she'd been kidnapped. He didn't have proof yet, but the signs were there. It was just a matter of time before the techs found something he could use to hunt her down.

He stared out the compound window. The desert blazed with morning sun, bright light reflecting off sand. It made him wince. He spun away and stalked back to her office.

It had to be in here. She'd been taken from *this* room, he felt it in his gut. And the answer had to start with her computer.

He crouched down under the desk and pulled out the hard drive.

Chapter 9

"**I**'m putting Dr. Sterling on the line. She'll give you all the pass codes she has and she'll walk you through her system protocol, but she says you will most likely find what you need in the Quadrant 3 computers. She suggests you focus technical time on that section."

"Why?" Sauvage's voice came through so clearly it felt as though he was in the room.

"Her work was being appropriated and weaponized without her knowledge and she has reason to believe it was done in Quadrant 3, which is where she hopes we'll find information about antidote stocks. She says she did create an antidote for the Ishonga pathogen that has been tested on chimps but not humans. She also said her pathogen was not tested on humans, either, at least not to her knowledge."

"It *was* tested—in Ishonga."

"Like I said, not to *her* knowledge."

"What about the president?"

"She has an idea which variation of the pathogen might have been used on him. But she has not developed an antidote for that one. Not yet."

Silence hung in the air.

Rafiq glanced sideways at Paige. She looked less like a brilliant scientist than a dusty street urchin in her oversized men's robes, and she'd never looked more endearing. "I believe her," he said.

"Put her on, then." If Rafiq believed her, so did they. "We have about five hours of download time left. As soon as we're done, pack that equipment up and get out of Na'jif. The men will rendezvous with you on the Saudi side of the Asir as arranged. The device you installed will self-destruct within thirty minutes of download completion. There will be no way to trace us."

"Affirmative."

Rafiq stood, held out his arm, motioned for Paige to seat herself in front of his equipment. He handed her the headset. Her eyes met his, and their gazes meshed. He touched her face gently, smiled. "Knock 'em dead, Doctor."

She returned his smile. A little wan, but brave, he thought. She'd had the stuffing knocked right out of her and she'd come up fighting. He had to admire that. In fact, he admired a hell of a lot about this woman. She was his kind of woman, someone who he could—

A soft rapping sounded on the door. Rafiq tensed, checked his watch, then relaxed. That would be the carpet dealer's mother with the brunch he'd ordered. He snagged his headcloth from the back of a chair and swung it over his head and mouth.

He unlocked the door, opened it cautiously. The dealer's mother stood there with the tray in her hands, but she was not alone. She was accompanied by three other women and a young girl of perhaps twelve. They'd been huddled in a group and whispering in hushed and excited tones as he opened the door, but they fell silent the instant they saw him.

They stared straight up at him in an openmouthed way that defied the current social and political climate. Rafiq's pulse kicked up a notch. There were no nervous hands, pulling veils over mouths. And worse, excitement danced in their dark eyes. It vibrated through them in a way that was literally palpable.

His heart began to pound. Word had gotten out. He should never have stared at Nahla's mother like that. He should *never* have gone down that road, back to that house. She must have said something. Rumors must be rustling through the city like a brush fire.

He drew his scarf higher, up over his nose. He and Paige had to leave town, or the sultan's army would be here within hours. The borders would start shutting down. Houses would be searched. The people who had helped him get into the country would be murdered.

Paige would be killed.

Sadiq would do whatever it took to keep the throne.

His little walk down memory lane yesterday may just have launched the revolution.

Rafiq took the tray from the woman and kicked the door closed. He stood with the tray, oblivious to what was on it.

He had a choice to make.

His actions had forced him to this point. Maybe he'd

even subconsciously wanted it to happen. He *was* going to fight this battle. He knew that now. He would stand up and face Sadiq, or die. But he could not allow it to cost this mission. He must finish that first.

He glanced up from the tray. Paige was still talking to Sauvage and his team. She'd put the headset on and was clicking away at his system.

He had to get her out of Hamān. Fast.

The weight of decision lay like a heavy mantle on his shoulders as he carried the tray into the room and set it on the small glass table.

She took the headset off and glanced up at him. A concerned expression crossed her face. "What's the matter? You look like you've just seen a ghost."

No, but the women at the door had. *He* was the bloody ghost, the one legend claimed was going to come back from the dead and save them.

She stood, came over to his side, touched his arm. "Are you okay, Rafiq?"

His eyes met hers, held. *Okay?* As okay as anyone who was about to officially come back from the dead and duel his half brother to the death.

Nervousness skittered through her features as she read his tension. "Did something just happen?"

"Nothing happened. Why don't you clean yourself up, dress in the *chador*. Put the jewelry back on, and use the kohl. I'm going to go down to the stable to make sure the camels and provisions are ready." He paused. "And eat some food."

She frowned. "I thought we were only going to leave after dark. The download isn't going to be complete until at least four."

"I want you ready. I want to leave Na'jif the very second the download is finished."

"In the daylight?"

"As soon as possible."

"Okay," she said studying him carefully. "But will you at least allow me to put some antibiotic ointment on that hand of yours. It's swelling and—" she smiled sheepishly "—human bites can be worse than animal ones."

He glanced at where she'd bitten him. He'd forgotten about it, and she was right; it was red and swelling, but there were more pressing things to worry about. "When I get back," he said, his words clipped. "Get dressed."

Paige was not going to put the *chador* on yet. It would be ludicrous to sit in the thing until four o'clock. She didn't know what had suddenly gotten Rafiq all edgy, but whatever it was, she was not going to cover herself until it was time to leave the safe house.

She had put on all the jewelry, though, and she'd painted her eyes heavily with kohl. Bells tinkled with each step as she walked out onto the patio carrying the jar of ointment and a bowl of hot water and soap.

Rafiq was pacing along the parapet, his stride angry and purposeful. He'd tied his hair back off his face with a leather thong, and it accentuated the sharp angle of his brows and the severity of his high cheekbones. He already had his tunic on and his *jambiya* at his waist. Rafiq looked as if he meant business. He looked predaceous. And proud, almost regal.

Paige stilled, watched him for a while. There was something very different about him. Something had definitely happened. Not once through her ordeal had she detected this kind of anticipatory edge in him. It made her nervous. She hadn't realized just how secure his powerful and calm confidence had made her feel, hadn't realized she needed it.

"Rafiq?" she called out to him as she set the bowl and disinfectant on the table.

He spun round, and his dark eyes flashed.

She patted the brocade of the chaise lounge. "Come sit here beside me. I'll fix that hand."

He checked his watch, shot a look at the Halliburton case and equipment. "Two more hours to go," he said. "Camels and supplies are waiting downstairs."

"That's plenty of time, Rafiq, come sit, I'll be quick. Bites like that can be lethal, trust me. I saw a guy lose his arm in the Congo because of a human bite that went septic."

He stalked over to the chaise lounge and sat next to her. This close, his energy was even more powerful, tangible.

Paige avoided the hot intensity in his eyes, dipped a cloth into the hot water and wrung it out. She dabbed at his skin. His eyes shot to hers with such a sudden ferocity that she hesitated, held her breath. But he said nothing, just stared into her eyes.

She swallowed, wiped the cloth over his wound, cleaning it, then drying it. He didn't move. He just skewered her with those eyes, and a muscle pulsed in his neck…at the same rate as her heart.

She looked away, moistened her lips, reached for the jar of ointment. She'd become overly conscious of her movements. She dipped her fingers into the slick ointment and began to smooth it over his skin, concentrating on avoiding his eyes. His skin was the color of rich coffee under her fingers. She could feel his pulse there, too, the rate matching hers. Her mouth went dry, and she found her hands lingering against his.

She cleared her throat. "There, that should do it." She looked up into his eyes again. The mystery in them sucked her in deeper than ever.

He lowered his thick lashes smokily. Dangerously. "Thank you, Doctor," he said, his voice thick.

She laughed lightly, a little too breathlessly. "I'm not that kind of doctor. And…I'm sorry I hurt you." She paused. "Thank you for coming after me, Rafiq…for believing in me."

His eyes flashed violently. He gripped her hands so fast and tightly she dropped the jar of ointment. It clattered to the tiles, rolled under the chair.

"Paige—" his voice was rough, low "—I *will* get you out. I promise you that. On my life."

She swallowed, suddenly unable to speak. The passion and ferocity in his grip, the brilliance in his eyes, wrapped around her, flowed through her, sparked a hot thrill deep in her belly.

He pulled her into him, pressed his mouth down over hers, cupped the back of her head with one hand, the other slipping down her spine to the base of her back and drawing her even closer. Shock and heat rippled through her. His lips moved over hers, hard, hungry, possessive. Heat speared through her, and her mind went completely blank. Her lips opened under his and she leaned into him, her breasts pushing up against his chest, heat spilling through her thighs, making her yearn to open totally, fully. He groaned, his tongue thrusting deep, searching—

A loud banging sounded on the door. His body snapped tight.

He pulled back, eyes flashing, his breathing ragged. "Paige—" he touched her cheek "—before everything changes—"

The banging intensified. A man started to yell. Rafiq's eyes shot toward the entrance hall.

She followed his look, suddenly frightened. "Before *what* changes, Rafiq?"

His eyes drilled back into hers. "No matter what happens, I *will* keep you safe. Believe in me, okay? Just promise me that."

Butterflies skittered through her stomach "Rafiq—"

He jerked to his feet, flung the cloth over his face, stalked to the door, one hand on the hilt of his *jambiya*.

Paige got up, followed him nervously at a distance.

He swung the door open.

The carpet dealer stood there, staring at Rafiq as if he were seeing him for the first time.

"What is it?" Rafiq asked, irritation clipping his voice.

"Why do you hide your face?"

Rafiq cursed. He reached out, took the man's arm, drew him into the apartment and locked the door behind him. "You know why," he said in a low voice. "I'm an exile. I'm a wanted man in this country. I do not wish to show my face to men who might betray me to the sultan."

"*I* will not betray you." There was challenge in the dealer's voice. Paige saw Rafiq's fingers closing around the hilt of his *jambiya*.

She took a step back. These two powerful men were squaring off, and she didn't know why. Her eyes flicked over to the desk. Rafiq had left his scimitar there.

"Show me your face." The Na'jif rebel boss threw down the gauntlet.

Paige edged backward toward the desk, toward the sword. If these men were going to fight, she might need a weapon.

"You have no need to see my face," Rafiq said. "It is

safer this way, for both you and me. They cannot torture you—or your family—if you have not seen me. You know this."

Paige's hip touched the desk. She kept her eyes trained on the two men as she fingered the smooth lacquered surface until her fingers connected with the cool hilt of the curved scimitar. She closed her hand around it, dragged it slowly toward her.

The dealer stood his ground, eyes fixed on Rafiq. Silence stretched taut, vibrated. The sounds of the city seemed to grow unnaturally loud, the midday heat heavy.

"It is true, isn't it?" the dealer said suddenly.

Rafiq did not answer.

"By Allah," the dealer whispered, his hand going to the gold symbol that hung from the thong at his neck. "It *is* true." There was a quiet awe, a reverence in his voice.

Paige stilled. Now she was really confused. What was true? She looked at Rafiq.

Still he said nothing. He stood erect, tension rolling off him in waves.

The dealer dropped suddenly to his knees, lowered his body as if in prayer and kissed the ground.

Paige's jaw dropped. What in hell was going on here?

He kneeled up, took Rafiq's hand in his, kissed that too. And Rafiq *let* him.

"*Rafiq bin Zafir bin Omar al-Qaadr,*" the dealer whispered. "The legend is true. The rightful heir has returned to lead us into battle. The king has returned." Tears filled his eyes, and he kissed the ground at Rafiq's feet again.

King! Paige dropped the sword. It clattered to the tiles at her feet. Neither man looked at her. They stared at each other, tension thick, vibrating, flowing out around them.

Rafiq slowly unwound his turban, let it drop to the ground.

The dealer watched, then bowed his head in silent reverence, tears flowing down his face. "It is true. It is true. It is true." He whispered over and over again. "Our people shall be saved. The battle starts."

Paige covered her mouth with her hand. Rafiq? *He* was the legendary savior? Her abductor was the rightful heir to the sultan's throne, the true sultan that the whole country had been waiting for all these years? It was not possible. How could it be?

A billion questions spiraled through her brain. She stared at his dark, arrogant profile. Was that *the* face—the image that all those women carried in little lockets tied to their waists hidden under their *chadors?* She'd never have recognized him. No one would. How could they? The images she'd seen were so old and so blurred and had been reproduced so many times on ancient black market equipment that it could have represented any Hamānian male. And the heir had been a young man when he'd fled the country fifteen years ago.

And he'd died in a battle with his half brother. Sadiq had killed Rafiq after he'd tried to slice his throat. There'd been a funeral. His father had attended.

So how come he lived? How come the true sultan was standing right here in front of her in pulsing flesh and blood, more alive and vital than any male she'd ever come across.

If this was true…she reached out, steadied herself against the desk as the implications began to sink in. If the true king really had returned, and word was out, that meant the revolution had started.

Her heart began to thud.

This was the sign the whole country had been waiting for. As word of the true king's return began to spread across the desert and into the cities, members of the Silent Revolution would be breaking open the underground arms caches, arming villagers, preparing to march on to the capital, to storm the palace and overthrow Sadiq and his corrupt regime.

The dealer got to his feet and stood in front of Rafiq with his head bowed. Where he'd once exuded confidence and authority, his posture was now one of subservience, in deference to his king.

And damned if Rafiq didn't look regal. He wore power as if he were born to it—which he was. This land belonged to him, the throne belonged to him. He was the rightful heir.

These were *his* people.

She couldn't quite get her head around it.

"I will bring the leaders of the rebel cells together at once," the dealer said. "We'll start coordinating with the cells in other villages and cities. We'll prepare for battle, praise the lord."

Rafiq placed his hand firmly on the man's shoulder. "No."

Disbelief rippled over the man's face. "What?"

Rafiq hesitated, and she realized he hadn't been ready for this. This was not part of his plan. So what *had* he been planning? A little question began to niggle at Paige. If he hadn't been killed by Sadiq, why had he left Hamān? Why had he deserted his people? Where had he been all this time when his nation had so clearly been suffering? Why had he hidden from power?

"No battle. Not yet," said Rafiq, his tone calm, but commanding.

"What do you mean, 'not yet'?" the dealer asked.

"We need a proper plan of attack. We cannot have a repeat of the Bin Ja'fir slaughter. The people were not prepared."

The dealer lifted his head, looked his king directly in the eye. "They *were*. They were prepared to die. For *you*. Sadiq had purged half his council. He'd killed everyone loyal to you, everyone who'd supported change. This was the act of a murderous autocrat. And the people of Bin Ja'fir were the first to rise in protest."

"And the last," said Rafiq. "We cannot let a massacre like that happen again. All the rebel cadres must be fully armed and they must be prepared to move in a coordinated fashion so that when we march on Al Qatar, the palace will fall swiftly. And all planning must be done in utmost secret, or the revolution will die before it starts."

Rafiq pressed his hand firmly down on the dealer's stalwart shoulder. "Which is why Sadiq *must not* know I am here. Not yet. You must help me leave the country at once. And you must quash the rumor that I have returned before it spreads beyond the walls of Na'jif."

The man stared at Rafiq, incredulity in his eyes. "This cannot be possible," he whispered. "We have waited for fifteen years for your return. We have prepared. You cannot leave us now." He shook his head. "Why? Why did you even come back if you are not ready to lead us?"

Rafiq raked his hand over his hair. Paige could see distress in the gesture. "I…needed to see firsthand what was happening in the country, so that I could go back and get that financing we spoke about. And the weapons. That has been my plan, and we must stick to it. I will be back with all the reinforcements we need. And I will come with the support of our neighbors and the international community. We must not go into battle ungirded fools. We cannot underestimate Sadiq's strength." He paused. "Or his hatred. And *that* is why I hide my face in Na'jif. I am not ready to show my presence. Not yet. And you *must* kill this rumor that I am back. I put my full faith in you. Lives will depend on this. Can you do this for me?"

The dealer stared at him. The seconds ticked by heavily. Finally, he bowed his head and spoke. "I am honored to do this for you, for our country."

She could see Rafiq's shoulders relax almost imperceptibly. "Thank you. You have harbored us well, and we are deeply grateful, but now we must leave. If you could make sure the way is clear? And make sure your mother lets everyone know she made an error in judgment?"

The man bowed lower and backed toward the door.

Rafiq let him out. He locked the door, but he stood facing it.

Paige walked up behind him.

"*You* are the sultan?"

He turned slowly, met her eyes. "I am the firstborn son of the first wife of Zafir bin Omar al-Qaadr. I am the rightful heir to Hamān."

Her jaw dropped. "So Sadiq is your half brother— you're the one who almost killed him?"

A hurricane of emotion ran through his eyes, and his fists clenched at his side. But he said nothing.

"Why did you do it? Why did you attack him? I thought he killed you."

"That's what they wanted the world to believe."

"And you let them get away with it? *Why?* Where did you go? Why did you hide? Do you know what happened after you disappeared? Do you know how many people were killed, how the country suffered?" She took a step toward him. "What made you run, Rafiq?"

He raised both hands. "Enough!" he barked. "Not now. Now we move."

"You cannot be serious? You can't possibly leave them now. Not again."

"I have a mission to complete," he snapped. "I must get you to safety."

"But Sadiq *will* hear of this, if he hasn't already. People could be taking up arms right now."

"I asked them to wait. They will."

"It's too late, Rafiq!" She stepped right up to him. "Don't you see? You *can't* leave them now! The war has started!"

He grabbed her arm, his grip like iron teeth in her skin. "Be quiet," he hissed. "We *must* leave. The balance of world power is at stake. I have a job to finish."

She jerked free of his hold. "Oh right, go save the world and watch your own people die. I don't think I can stand to watch it."

He glowered at her.

She glared back. "You lied to him, didn't you? You told the dealer you were coming back. If you really intended on coming back, you would've done it years ago."

"I did not lie. It's the truth."

She gave a soft snort. "Yeah, right. You're a coward, you know that? You're a coward who deserted your people the first time, and you're doing it again."

His face turned to black thunder. His brows lowered and he began to shake. He pointed his finger at her face. "Do not presume to pass judgment on something you know nothing about." He leaned closer, getting his face right into hers, his voice growling like low smoke through a ravine. "Prejudice, Dr. Sterling, is an evil in itself. And you, as a scientist, should know better."

She held her ground, looked him square in the eye. "Then why don't you explain it to me, Rafiq? Why don't you tell me what really happened?"

"Because," he said slowly, "it's none of your business."

"Then how the hell am I supposed to understand you?"

"You're not." He stood to his full height, looked down at her. "And I don't need your approval."

His words hit her in the gut. They hurt. A hell of a lot more than they should have. Paige stared at him. He'd come to save her before he gave his men the codes. He'd protected her at the risk of his mission. He'd kissed her. He *had* to care what she thought. Didn't he? Had she totally misjudged, misread everything about him?

An alarm screamed from the computer.

Paige gasped, whirled around.

Rafiq lurched toward the system, jabbed a few keys. The terrible screeching sound died. He hit another key. "Sauvage!"

Silence.

"*Sauvage!* Come in!"

"Zayed!" Just one word and the tension could be cut with a knife.

"The alarm sounded. What's going on?"

Paige could hear tense voices in the background. "I'm putting December on."

A man with a deep and resonant African accent spoke. "We've been compromised, Zayed. The transmitting device has begun to self-destruct."

"But...the download is not complete."

"The process has been halted. I believe the device has been found."

Rafiq cursed violently in Arabic. "How is that possible? I thought no electronic trace would lead back to the hard drive on which it was installed."

"This had to have been detected manually. Someone opened her hard drive, and searched specifically for it."

"Could it have malfunctioned, perhaps, started to self-destruct early?"

"It's possible, but not likely," said December.

Paige came to his side. "What now?" she whispered.

He looked at her. "Now the bio-bomb goes off."

Silence hung heavy.

Her heart began to pound.

She turned to look at the screen, watched the electronic clock ticking down the seconds. "How…how soon?" she whispered.

"God alone knows. We'll monitor intelligence channels, watch news wires. It's all we can do for now. Wait. And pray."

Paige felt sick. "Can't you alert anyone? Get the cities to evacuate?"

"If by chance the device did self-destruct, alerting federal emergency teams would show the Cabal that the president had engaged outside help. That could, in itself, launch the attack. And we don't have an antidote. We don't even know how it will be released. Evacuating the cities could just end up spreading the disease faster throughout the entire country. We'll know soon enough if they're on to us."

By the first deaths.

Dizziness spiraled. The heat weighed down on her. Paige pressed her hands to her forehead. He was right. They'd have to quarantine rather than evacuate. They'd have to hold everyone *in* the cities. And if people knew what was coming, they'd try to flee. It would be chaos. They'd have to bring in the National Guard to hold back the citizens, if the soldiers didn't flee themselves. And the violence…. Oh God, they *needed* that antidote. It was the *only* hope.

She grabbed Rafiq's shoulder. "Get me out of Hamān! If you guys don't find an antidote stock, I can start working on creating some. This disease *will* spread, and it *will* be terrible, but if state emergency measures can contain it to the key cities we *may* be able to halt a worldwide pandemic. Get me out, Rafiq. Now."

"She's right," said Sauvage. "Leave Hamān, *mon ami.* At once. And bring the doctor in. If we don't find what we need in the download data we do have, she and Meyer are going to have to get to work. It's the best we can do now."

Rafiq hit the button, cut off communication. He slapped the case shut, scooped up wires. "Go!" he yelled as he worked. "Camels are saddled and prepared in the court-yard. I'll meet you there."

Paige grabbed her *chador* and ran for the door while Rafiq cleared up the rest of the equipment.

13:00 Charlie, Sultan's Palace, Al Qatar, Hamānian capital, Friday, October 4

The bell over his bed sounded. Sultan Sadiq bin Zafir Omar al-Qaadr cursed softly. Then chose to ignore the bell. He traced his fingers slowly over the young woman's rounded breast. She lay naked in front of him, legs splayed, her dark hair spread over his silk pillows. He found her nipple, rolled it tightly between his fingers.

Was that brightness in her eyes fear? A smile curled

slowly over his lips. He liked the mix of pain braided with pleasure. It made him so hard and so hot it hurt. It made his body scream for release. He ran his tongue over his teeth, leaned over her, his chest pushing up against the tightness of her breasts.

The bell clanged again.

Damn the fools! Did they want to risk their lives?

He jerked up from the bed, snatched his silk robe from the bedpost, cinched the sash over his waist, and strode to his chamber door. He flung it open, words of fury on his lips.

It was his chief counsel, anxiety in his eyes.

The words of anger died on Sadiq's lips. Worry wormed its way into his heart. "What is it?" he demanded.

His counsel hesitated. Sadiq's heart beat faster. "Speak! You keep me from my rest!"

"It…it is probably just a rumor, Your Majesty. You know how these things are. It cannot be true. It…it's just not possible."

Sadiq stepped out of his chambers, closed the door quietly behind him, glanced down the corridors. "*What* is just a rumor?" he hissed.

"Rafiq. He…your half brother is back."

Chapter 10

The man squinted into the glare that bounced off the sand. Even behind shades, his pale eyes burned. It was the curse of scant pigment, but physical discomfort was something he'd learned to register only in a very distant part of his brain. What snared his attention now were the military troops that appeared to be surrounding the walled city of Na'jif.

He slowed his horse.

Na'jif was one of three cities within possible radius of the wireless transmitting device he'd found planted in Dr. Sterling's computer. And he'd discovered camel prints outside the perimeter fence that led in this direction. His quarry had headed to Na'jif, he was certain of it. And now something was going down.

A cadre of soldiers began to gallop toward him on

camels, dust churning behind them. His pulse quickened. He didn't speak the language and he hadn't brought a translator. He couldn't afford to be arrested now. It would take forever to get through the red tape.

He did have the requisite travel papers, authorized by the sultan himself. But he also had a satellite phone. Any phone was illegal. And he carried a concealed firearm. That, too, was against the law. His travel documents made that clear. He'd have to ditch those, use his knife when it came down to the kill.

The soldiers were coming straight for him.

He dismounted quickly, dropped to his knees and buried his phone and gun. He took the reins and pressed innocently forward to meet the soldiers on foot, knowing he would appear less of a threat that way.

His employer in Manhattan would not be able to contact him now. But that didn't matter. He never spoke to anyone until his job was complete. Manhattan could wait.

Twenty minutes later, he was corralled outside the city walls with other travelers, under the guard of nervous young soldiers. Their coordination was patchy. Something major was going down, and he could sense the troops weren't all on the same page. Some of the men looked afraid, others excited.

He managed to find one who could speak some English and he asked why he was being held. The soldier told him it was a precaution. There was a rumor blowing through the land that a man who claimed to be the true king had returned to take back the throne. Civil war would break out if the sultan's army did not find and apprehend the imposter within the next few hours. All travelers in and out of the city were being stopped.

"Are you sure he is an imposter?" he asked.

The young soldier looked wary. He glanced over his shoulder to see who else might be listening. "It is the sultan's word that he is." The soldier explained that villagers under duress had told the militia that the "imposter" had ridden into Na'jif with a fair-skinned woman on Thursday morning. The woman had not been wearing a regulation *chador,* and they were thought to be hiding somewhere in the walled city.

"Take me to your commander, at once," he said.

"Why?"

"I can help you find this man." *And the woman.*

19:20 Charlie, Na'jif plateau, Friday, October 3

For five hours they'd raced in a straight line toward the purple foothills of the Asir—two camels, robes flying—over the undulating ripples of sand as far as the eye could see.

The sun burned down hot on their backs as it curved in its arc toward the Red Sea, but not once did they slow their brutal pace.

The sound of the camels' hooves on sand thudded through his veins, and Rafiq's heart began to pound with the ancient blood of his warrior ancestors. Each mile over the desert stripped back another layer, another barrier of the past fifteen years; each hour under the unrelenting Arabian sun exposed the raw and fierce Bedouin pride that burned deep inside.

And the strong woman keeping pace at his side fed his energy, his strength, his purpose, his spirit. Feeling her racing alongside him fired his blood, his desire to fight, to reclaim his country. Paige Sterling was a woman who could handle this terrain—a woman who could handle him.

She was a woman worthy of a king.

Shock rippled through him at the thought, and he quashed it instantly. He had to focus on getting her out of Hamān, not keeping her for himself.

Why would she want a life with him, anyway? She was his polar opposite. They lived in different worlds. How could he even entertain the idea?

And his road ahead was going to be hard and bloody. He might not survive. He had no business thinking about trying to build a future with her, with anyone. Not until he'd liberated his country.

Besides, she thought him a *coward*.

Perhaps he was.

He slowed his camel to a stop as the sun sank below the horizon in a fiery orange ball, throwing shadows behind every little ridge of sand. They'd reached the steep western escarpment and the jagged ridges of the Asir loomed above them.

Paige brought her camel to a stop next to his. She was breathing hard and her kohl-rimmed eyes were bright, fierce with the energy of their flight, a mirror of his own passions. It lit something in him just to look at her. God, she really was beautiful. And at this very minute he wanted her, more than anything.

"Which way do we go now?" she asked.

He didn't have a clue which way to go with her, how to handle the complexities of what he was feeling at the moment. He just knew he had to get her to safety. That was the first step.

"That way." He pointed up into the darkening crevices. "We need to go through that narrow pass between those two mountains. It leads to a route down to the Saudi-Yemeni border on the other side. We'll travel until dark, then we can rest and water the camels."

She squinted up at the peaks. "Is that the way you came through?"

"Yes. Hamānian airspace is completely closed. I was dropped off by chopper on the Saudi side, where I had a guide waiting with a camel. It's the shortest route through the Asir."

He nudged his camel forward carefully picking a route through rocks of sharp flint. "Stones are loose, so watch your footing."

And they began their climb in silence.

They slowly worked their way up the steep, winding path as the sky turned indigo and the air began to cool. Paige could smell pine. Her camel made soft snorting noises, and a pot clanked gently against a tin mug strapped to one of her saddlebags.

The path flattened out along a narrow ridge crowded with twisted juniper trees. It was getting dark and difficult to see, only the stars and a rising sickle moon lighting the way. Rafiq halted his beast on the ridge ahead of her, motioned for her to stop.

They'd climbed incredibly high already. The land of Hamān seemed to stretch out from the foothills below them, an expanse of sand, and rolling dunes all the way to the Red Sea.

He took out a pair of night vision binoculars and scanned the plateau they'd just spent the better part of the day traversing.

She saw him tense.

Paige squinted, trying to see what he'd seen, but it was too dark. She edged her camel closer to his. "What is it?"

He handed her the binoculars. The move, the trust, surprised her. He was treating her as an equal, a partner. She took the scopes from him, put them to her eyes, adjusted the vision.

"I...can't really see anything, other than maybe a bit of a windstorm brewing."

"That's no windstorm. Those are soldiers."

"Following us? Already?"

"The goddamn army."

Her stomach tightened. She lowered the binoculars. "You think it's the Land Command?"

"No. That'd be the sultan's armed forces. Horses. Armored vehicles. Munitions."

Her eyes met his. They glinted in the dim light. "He knows. About you."

He nodded.

The pace of her heart quickened. "I told you, Rafiq. It's too late to run. You *have* to fight. The war has started."

"I am not running," he snapped. "I *will* be back."

She said nothing. She could see now that the man was caught between a rock and one hell of a hard place. She had no idea why he'd left his country in the first place, but she could also see now how vital it was to get that antidote made.

He took the scopes from her, lifted them to his eyes, peered into the dusk. A cool wind was beginning to rush down the mountain, displacing the hot desert air, beginning to whip the ends of their robes.

"They're still several hours out. If they know we headed toward the Asir, they'll be heading for the pass. It's the most logical route into Saudi Arabia. And they'll likely have reinforcements grouping along the Saudi side of the mountains.

"So we're *trapped?*"

He spun in his saddle, secured the scopes, nudged his camel around and urged it onto a barely visible path that snaked along the ridge. "We go south, this way. They'll expect us to head east, over that pass. They'll follow it to the end looking for our tracks. It'll buy us time."

Her camel automatically followed his. Paige was nervous riding in the dark, especially on such a narrow steep trail.

"We'll find somewhere to lay low tonight," he called back to her, "until the cadre has passed. Then before dawn, we'll backtrack behind them, up to another path that will take us through the peaks to the south, closer to Yemen. Yaah," he said softly, urging his camel to move faster along the treacherous ridge, using the cover of the juniper forest to hide their progress.

They moved like that for another hour, the air growing cooler, the breeze fragrant with the scent of juniper trees. He stopped suddenly in front of her. "Over there, around that ridge, see?"

A strange dark bulk rose out and over the rocks and blotted the faint milky stars that spattered the sky.

"What is it?" she asked coming up alongside him.

"Ruins of a Crusader castle. Probably eleventh century."

A strange sense of timelessness filled Paige as she studied the dark hulking shape of the castle ruins on the ridge. She and Rafiq were treading on ground that had been traversed by people hundreds and hundreds of years ago. The sense of spiritual awe was so powerful that it brought tears to her eyes.

Rafiq leaned over, brushed her cheek with the backs of his fingers. "Hey, you okay?"

She nodded in silence, wanting to lean into him, to feel him next to her, to share the sensation she couldn't begin to articulate.

"What is it?" he whispered in Arabic.

She drew in a deep breath. "It's…just the idea that knights and Moors traveled this very path so many hundreds of years ago, under those same stars, using the same mode of transport as we are." She smiled softly and looked into his eyes. "It kind of makes me feel insignificant in the scope of it all. It makes you question what you really want from your own little slice of life on earth."

He remained silent for a while, with just the soft rush of wind in juniper leaves and the snorts of their camels in the night air.

"What *do* you want, Paige?" He finally asked, his voice quiet, serious.

She bit her lip. She wasn't sure anymore. She was on a cusp—her old life destroyed, the future an unknown landscape, both frightening and exciting. "All I know is…that I just don't want to do it all alone anymore," she whispered softly.

He studied her in the dark. But he said nothing.

He turned his camel suddenly and headed up the path, sending small rocks clattering far down into the canyon.

Something slipped in her stomach, and she felt incredibly alone. She watched Rafiq moving ahead of her like an ancient Moorish warrior. And she realized it was him she wanted. It was a ridiculous notion. And once she got back to civilization, she'd realize it was a heat-of-the-moment thing.

Besides, he was a sultan. He had a war to fight, a country to reclaim, princesses to marry.

Who did she think she was, anyway? A man like him didn't lack for women. A man like him chose women for political purpose. He used them to build alliances with neighboring countries.

Besides, she really knew very little about him—such as why he deserted Hamān in the first place.

They neared the stone walls, the shape of the crumbling turrets taking form against the pale moonlight, the sheer size of the place becoming evident.

He brought his camel to a stop. "We can hole up in the castle grounds tonight and water the animals."

And defend themselves from the bastions if necessary. But that notion hung unspoken between them.

Paige dismounted, led her camel through an ancient arch, feeling as if she were crossing through a portal from one world to another, feeling as if she was no longer Dr. Paige Sterling, but just a woman in time. She stopped for a moment to gather herself, allowing Rafiq to go ahead before following him into the castle courtyard where the air was still and eerie. Grass grew thick around an old well. She let her camel go and he made straight for it, began nosing at it with happy snuffling sounds. She smiled in spite of herself. The horror of the pathogen and a world on the brink of war seemed a million miles and as many light years away.

Rafiq sat up near a turret and punched Sauvage's number into his satellite phone as he watched Paige in the courtyard below him. She'd taken off her *chador* and her hair gleamed almost silver in the moonlight. He watched as she lit a fat tallow candle and placed it in a stone alcove. She was now laying out a blanket.

"Zayed?" The voice startled him back. He glanced quickly through the narrow slit in the wall, making sure the desert plains far below were still empty. The sand in this region was pale and it reflected the light of the moon. Any army would stick out a mile away. They'd be safe here for a while. "*C'est moi.* What's the news?"

"Still nothing. No sign the Cabal has been alerted."

"So you think it was a technical glitch?"

"I don't know. December thinks it's unlikely. Perhaps someone found the device—a Nexus employee like Sterling, unaware of Cabal motives, or even its existence. It may take a while for the news to filter up. The bombs could still blow."

"Well we can do with a small reprieve." He hesitated.

"It may take us a day longer than anticipated to get out of here."

"Why?"

"The sultan has mobilized his army. We have troops tracking us. We can no longer cross the Saudi border. We need pickup on the Yemeni side."

"*What?* The sultan is involved?"

Rafiq sucked in his breath. He had to tell him. It was going to come out one way or another. "This has nothing to do with the Cabal. He wants me."

"Zayed—"

He closed his eyes for a moment. There was no simple way to say this. "I am the true king of Hamān."

Dead silence stretched through space.

Sauvage laughed, breaking the silence. "You been chewing the qat, eh?"

Rafiq said nothing.

"This is *true?* You're telling me the sultan of Hamān is…your half brother?"

"I am Rafiq bin Zafir bin Omar al-Qaadr, the rightful heir to the Hamānian monarchy. According to the constitution, if I return—"

"*Merde!*" he hissed. "How does the sultan *know* you are there?"

"Someone recognized me." Rafiq hesitated. "The entire nation has been waiting for me. The rebels have been amassing arms."

Sauvage swore again, softly, but no less violently. "This is not a minor problem, *non?* You have started a rebellion. A civil war."

Rafiq watched Paige drawing water out of the old well for the camels, the sight of her strangely soothing to his mind.

She was the only thing real and tangible thing in his world right at this moment—a muse with a conscience. One that was guiding him right now, keeping his focus on what was important.

"It will not be a problem," he said calmly. "My mission remains the same. Always has." It was a lie. Nothing was the same. But then again, it was. The circle had come together. "I'll let you know when we get near the Yemeni border."

"We won't be able to send air support into Yemen. We have no arrangement with the government."

"We will have to exit by sea, across from Djibouti. Can you get a boat into the Gulf of Aden for us? An old fishing vessel, maybe? We won't attract attention that way."

"That can be arranged. We can have the chopper pick Sterling up from the boat, and we can have a jet on standby in Djibouti to fly her into São Diogo, ASAP."

Rafiq signed off, walked out along the crumbling parapet and stared over the land. *His* land. A strange exhilaration blew over him with the night breeze.

He heard Paige coming along the parapet, the clink of her bells and bracelets incredibly feminine. She came up behind him, touched his shoulder so gently that he caught his breath, and with it, her scent. Warmth and power rushed through his veins.

"Rafiq, look at me."

He turned slowly. Moonlight shimmered in her silver eyes. She moved closer and his gut tightened, his body braced. He felt hot.

"What's the news?"

"No attack. Not yet. They may not even be aware the device is related."

"Thank God," she whispered. She stood beside him, her arm brushing his, and stared out over his desert. He could almost feel her mind reaching into space, thinking; she never stopped thinking. What was she thinking now?

She lifted her face to his suddenly. "Let me go, Rafiq. Alone."

"What?"

"Tell me the way, give me a camel and supplies, and let me try and make it over the mountains on my own. You stay here. Help your people."

Shock rippled through him. "You won't make it alive. Not alone."

"I might. And if I don't, at least I'll die trying. The loss of my life won't be the end of the world, Rafiq."

It'll be the end of mine. She'd just made him see it, right this minute—clear as moonlight over white desert.

"If I don't make it, your techs have my pass codes, they know how to access my system, my research. Dr. Meyer is the best there is. He can use—"

"No!" He gripped her by the shoulders. "I *cannot* let you go alone. Meyer will work faster with your help, your guidance."

"There's an entire army after us, Rafiq. What chance do

either of us have of getting over the border? It's not me they want. It's *you*. They don't know anything about the pathogen or the antidote. This is *your* battle. Let me go and fight mine. I'll have a better chance of getting out if the army isn't after me."

He hated the fact her argument made sense. But he didn't want to let her go for reasons that went deeper than any logic.

"Paige, I can't…I can't let you—"

She reached slowly up, removed the cloth that covered his head, dropped it to the ground. She feathered his jaw with her fingers. His heart melted into his stomach, and his brain turned to molasses.

"You belong here, Rafiq," she whispered. "And I'm sorry for what I said."

"That I'm a coward?"

"I don't know why you left Hamān, but I think I've come to know enough about you to believe that it had to be for a damn good reason."

Rafiq closed his eyes, the sweet pain almost too much. There was no disapproval in her voice. No explanation needed from him. Just her understanding. His chest ached sharply. In some way, it felt as if she'd just given him absolution— the absolution he hadn't even known he'd needed so badly— absolution that had to come from the lips of a woman like her.

A woman who could compare to his Nahla.

In that instant, he wanted Paige Sterling more than anything in the world. He couldn't even begin to find the words. And here, in her understanding, in her *acceptance* of him, she was pointing out they had two different roads to travel. And he knew damn well that they'd never meet again if he let her go now. He wasn't prepared to do this. This was not the best way.

"Rafiq." Her voice grew grave, insistent. She really meant it. This woman had embraced his mission. She'd made it hers. And she'd set him free to settle his past. It was an overwhelming gift.

"Tell Sauvage I'm coming alone. Have his men meet me. Tell him I must do this, because it's my fault—"

He cupped her face tightly in his hands. "No, Paige! This is *not* your fault!" He drew her body up to his, brought his lips close to her mouth, his hunger for her all-consuming. "You were *used,* Paige. Like Nahla."

She went dead still, and her eyes widened.

Rafiq threw his head back to the sky and swore softly. He hadn't meant to say that. Not now.

"Was that her name?" Paige asked.

He inhaled sharply, leveled his head, looked into her eyes. "Yes, that was her name."

"Tell me, Rafiq," she said gently, touching his face. "Tell me what happened all those years ago."

*22:07 Charlie, Venturion penthouse, Manhattan,
Friday, October 3*

He consulted his watch. It was just after 3 p.m. in New York, and still no word from his man in Hamān. He paced restlessly along the length of the floor-to-ceiling windows, the lights of the city blurred by rivulets of autumn rain.

He was in the dark, in more ways than one.

His hit man had made it clear he never wanted to be bothered while on a job. Ever. He'd once said you can't make a cat stalk faster once he has sighted his prey. You just had to wait. The kill would happen when the time was right.

But this time was different. His man did not know what was really at stake here, nor did he want him to know.

He grabbed a bottle of mineral water, twisted the cap off. He was losing control. He *had* to find out what was happening in Hamān. He swigged the water, stared at his reflection against the black pane.

He had to do it. He had to call his man.

He set the bottle down and reached for the phone, the special phone. He punched in the number, moistened his lips, waited…and waited. And waited.

No answer.

His heart began to race. His mouth turned dry. He quickly punched the number in again.

And somewhere in the sands of Hamān a phone rang under the stars.

Chapter 11

Rafiq took a deep breath. "Nahla was my fiancée."

Surprise rippled through Paige. "I…I had no idea you were going to be married."

"Not many people did know. She was not my family's choice for queen. Nahla was from Na'jif, and she was not born of royalty. She was—" he looked up at the night sky "…from the wrong side of the tracks, I guess you'd say." He stilled, turned to look right into her eyes. "Do you believe in love at first sight, Paige?"

She studied the shadows of his face. "There's scientific basis for lust at first sight."

Rafiq laughed. "Is it always like this with you, always about science and logic? Never about the heart?"

She looked away. "I never really thought about it. I think I'm afraid, of being hurt, abandoned." She shook her head. "I think I shut down when my parents vanished. I don't know that I ever really opened up again." She shivered in the cool breeze.

He put his arm around her, drew her into his arms, and together they gazed out over the desert.

"Was it like that with Nahla?" she asked after a while. "Love at first sight?"

"It was. I was nineteen, and I knew the minute I saw her in the market that I wanted her to be my queen. My *only* queen."

Paige smiled. "That would have made you something of a revolutionary, given your country's history of many wives for one sultan."

He shrugged. "I was what my father called forward-thinking. And he embraced that in me, even groomed it. It's why he sent me to Europe, to study global politics, law and economics at the Sorbonne. You see, he knew Hamān, as one of the last absolute monarchies in the world, could not continue to remain isolated. Our only trade, our only outside contact was with the Soviet Union, and with the demise of the Soviet empire, he knew we would have to start looking outward. He had high hopes that I would be the one to lead the country into the future, into global alliance, trade and even democracy."

"Your father had that vision?"

"Yes, but where there is visionary thinking, there is also resistance. Much of the old-school council opposed the concept of change. They believed instead in upholding radical fundamentalist beliefs and archaic Bedouin custom. And that meant there was also opposition to *me*. And the fact that I was in line to take the throne did not sit well with my half brother, Sadiq. He was older, aggressive and power-hungry, and he wanted the throne for himself. But he was only second in the line of succession, being the first son of my father's second wife. I was the first son of the first wife."

"What happened with Nahla?"

"My father grew ill, and his mind and will grew weak. He started caving to the opposition. He said if we wanted to keep doing things our way, we would have to go slowly, and I would have to appease the council by keeping my relationship with Nahla secret. He said my transition to sultan would be easier that way. But I knew that he hoped I would simply forget about my 'infatuation' while studying in Europe."

"You didn't."

"Of course not. Our love just grew stronger. We wrote daily…" He fell silent for a while; the only sound was a slight whistle of wind up in the turrets. "We had great dreams for the nation, Nahla and I."

Paige felt a strange twinge she could only interpret as a feeling of envy. To be so deeply loved by a man like Rafiq… "What attracted you to her, that day you first saw her?"

He smiled in the dark, his teeth glinting in the faint moonlight. "It was her vitality, the passion that danced in her eyes. And she was beautiful, in a natural, totally unaffected way. She also had brains and a vision that I came to love." He glanced down at her. "You see, Paige, Nahla, too, was a revolutionary thinker. She had organized a small rally that confronted me when I visited Na'jif. I had been traveling around Hamān, getting to know the cities and towns, my future subjects." He laughed softly. "And she wanted to let the future king know that the country needed to change."

"*She* organized a protest?"

"You have to remember, even back in those days, it was better for Hamānian women than now. They were not obligated to cover themselves, they could work outside the home, they could travel freely."

"And that's when you fell in love with her, that day?"

"Absolutely. I courted her before I left for Europe and during my vacations. And I got to know her deeply through her letters. And the more I discovered, the more I wanted her to be my wife."

Paige clutched her arms over her stomach, against the chill, against what she suspected was coming next. "Sadiq did something terrible, didn't he?"

"Sadiq went into action in my final year of university, at the time my father was given only months to live. Sadiq had been courting the radical opposition faction for some time in a bid to stir trouble with me, and when he found out about Nahla—" a tremor ran through his body "—he did the unthinkable. And he did it to destroy me in the most fundamental way."

"*He...killed her?*"

Rafiq tensed. "Cold-blooded murder wouldn't have allowed Sadiq to become sultan under terms of the rules of succession. He found another way to destroy me, worse than death." He stepped away from Paige, spun round, his eyes glittering fiercely in the moonlight. "He went to Na'jif. He dragged Nahla out into the desert and forced himself on her." His voice cracked. "He knew it would set in motion a chain of events that would destroy us both."

Paige felt sick. She knew that rape in Hamān had always

been considered the woman's fault. Nahla would have been doomed. It would have fallen on the men in her family to take her life, or the entire family would be shamed and forever shunned, destroyed both economically and socially.

She raised her hand to touch his face, stopped. She didn't know what to do, how to ease the pain of his memory. She wished she hadn't asked.

"What…what happened to her, Rafiq?"

"She wanted to save her family from shame. And she knew her chances of marrying me would be over. Hamānian law would not let me rule if the council learned I planned to take a wife that had been…. She took her own life, Paige. The night before I returned to Na'jif with a ring in my pocket."

Rage began to shake in Paige's limbs. "So no one outside her family circle, and you, ever found out about Sadiq raping her?"

"No!" His eyes glistened. "My father was the only other person who knew. Nahla protected her family from shame and ruin. She protected my right to succession."

She placed her hand on his arm. "Oh, Rafiq, I…I don't know what to say. I don't know how you could have borne the pain…the hatred—"

"I *didn't*," he said through clenched teeth. "I rode through the night to Al Qatar. I stormed into Sadiq's palace quarters. I found the bastard in bed with another woman, one of his *wives*. I was blind with fury. I hauled him naked from his bed, and I started to slice his throat with my sword. I wanted it slow. I wanted to watch his eyes. I wanted to feed off his terror and feel his blood flow hot over my hands. But his wife screamed and fetched the palace guards, and they hauled me off him."

He was silent, trembling. He looked at her, deep. "I have never spoken of this. Ever. Not since that night."

"Is that when you fled the country?"

He nodded. "I wanted nothing more to do with Hamān. I think what was worse than not being able to kill Sadiq that night was having my father tell me I must just forget about what happened. He said I must protect my right to succession. He said if the council found out about Nahla, they would challenge my right to rule, and Sadiq would become king. Even in his weak state, my father did not want that."

"And you told him to screw it."

He actually smiled. He touched her cheek. "You're good for me, you know that, Paige? Talking about this…it feels a little easier. And yeah, I told the old man to go to hell. I told him I wanted nothing to do with a country, a culture or a family that could endorse what Sadiq had done. I wanted to excise the whole damn place from my soul. I told him I was leaving, that Sadiq could have the throne, that they could all get what they deserved. My father was furious. He said if I left, I would be as good as dead to Hamān. He said he would claim I had died in battle with Sadiq, and he would hold a funeral for me. Because if Hamānians ever learned I had walked out on him and the council, there would be civil war. I told him to go ahead, do what he liked."

He stood silent a while, looking out over the desert. "I never saw him again, Paige. He died the day after I left the country, and Sadiq took his throne."

"Where did you go?"

"That part you know. I joined the French Foreign Legion, where a man can bury his past and earn a new identity."

"Perhaps, Rafiq, it was your destiny to do so."

His eyes flashed to hers. "Do you believe that ridiculous legend?"

She smiled. "I'm a scientist, remember, I'm not supposed to believe in that stuff. But these things do grow out of kernels of truth. Perhaps there was a leak that you did not really die. And that you might come back. I don't think you can ever underestimate the power of hope, Rafiq."

"I suppose you're right."

She shivered against the chill again.

He took her hand. "Come, let us go back down, out of the wind. You must try and sleep a while. There is still a long ride ahead."

He led her down the crumbling steps, stopped at the bottom. "Perhaps *you* are my destiny, Paige. This mission—you—forced me to look into my past again." He looked into her eyes. "And I want you to know that I will *not* turn my back on Hamān. I just have to get you to safety first, and then I will come back."

"I—"

"No." He placed his fingers softly over her lips. "I *have* to do this first. Getting you out, saving a woman I care about, deeply, a woman that has been used by a system that is evil—*that* will be my absolution, Paige. *My* way of rectifying the past, of protecting the future. And you can no more deny me that than deny me my soul. It is who I am."

And in that moment, Paige knew she'd fallen in love with the sultan of Hamān.

Paige couldn't sleep. She lay beside Rafiq, listening to him breathe, replaying his story in her mind, her feelings for him deepening each time she did.

A love like the one he had for Nahla…it went beyond sexual, beyond hormones and body chemistry. It was spiritual. Sublime. It was something she didn't understand, and something a woman could only dream about. Especially sharing it with a man like Rafiq. He had such a magnetic physical presence, such male power. Her body went warm just thinking about it, about him.

She *had* to ask. Her mind was not going to let this rest. She propped herself up on her elbow. "Rafiq…did…did you date many women after…I mean did you sleep with anyone after—"

He laughed softly. "I slept with plenty of women after I left Hamān. I drank too. I did all the things I never did in my own country. It was my way of thumbing a nose at a culture and heritage that had betrayed me."

All the things he never did in his own country. "You…you mean you never made love with Nahla?"

"I never slept with anyone while I was waiting for her, either."

Paige flopped back onto the blanket. That *was* love. "You were a virgin," she said to the sky.

He laughed again, low and smoky and wicked. And so very sexy that she flushed. She was embarrassed for even allowing her mind to go there. She started to sit up, suddenly needing a bit of distance from him, cool air on her face.

But he held her down, and he traced his finger over her face, from her brow, along her cheekbone, down to her jaw, and around until it rested on her bottom lip. She felt her mouth open under the subtle pressure, and heat spilled into her belly.

He moved his finger inside her lip, ran it slowly along the exquisitely sensitive seam. "I made up for it." he said with a low whisper, teasing her with his smile. "I made love to every woman I felt like seducing." He pushed her lip open a little further, and she tasted the salt of him on her tongue.

He leaned over her, his lips close to hers, his eyes watching hers, and he moved his finger harder against her tongue. Paige felt her vision begin to swim.

"I drank what I liked." His voice curled through her, and in a part of her brain she registered that he'd switched to soft, guttural Arabic. "I indulged in every sensual pleasure that came my way, embraced it as a connoisseur. I found physical pleasure." He traced her teeth with his finger, pushing a little harder, and she curled her tongue around him, teasing him back, testing, tasting, slipping, her breathing becoming ragged, her belly hot.

"But not once, Paige, did I ever make love with my heart," he whispered against her ear, his breath hot in the cool night air. "Never with my mind. Only with the physical senses. Existing in the now. And making love that way can be pure primal pleasure, Paige." He leaned forward, whispered over her lips. "Have you ever tried it that way, Paige?" The blood drained completely from her head, and she began to throb down below.

Then she registered what he'd just said. She struggled to find her mind, her will, to fight her way back. She pushed his hand away, sat up, hurt in her heart, tears in her eyes.

"You can't seduce me, Rafiq." The huskiness in her voice betrayed her.

He leaned forward, brushed her lips with is. "Is that a challenge, Doctor?" he murmured.

"I…" She felt her insides melt. It was biological reaction. She knew exactly what was happening to her body, where the blood was making her hot and swollen, how her breasts were responding to his words, his touch…and her mind was fading, the world receding to this instant alone.

"Because I know I can arouse you. I've seen it in your eyes, Doctor. I have felt it in your lips. The cerebral scientist is not beyond physical pleasure is she?"

"No," she whispered. Aching. Feeling more human and alive and more conflicted than she ever had in her life.

Then suddenly she pushed back, her mind clearing. She did *not* want this. Not after hearing about Nahla, of the depth of love this man was capable of. She didn't want to be just a physical sensation to him, like all the women he'd bedded over the last fifteen years. But what *did* she want. More? Emotion? True love? This was garbage. Stupid. It was a reaction to stress. For both of them.

She jerked to her feet, her eyes filling with hot emotion. What in hell was this sultan-warrior doing to her?

"Paige?"

She said nothing. She left him sitting on the blanket and crossed the courtyard, scrambled up stairs and climbed up to the parapet. She placed her hands on the stone wall, looked out over the moonlit plains and let the evening breeze wash the emotion from her face.

And suddenly he was behind her, arms around her, mouth under hair at her shoulder, breath in her ear.

Her legs turned boneless in spite of herself.

"Damn you, Rafiq," she whispered. "Please, leave me alone. I—" Her voice cracked. She pulled away, kept her face turned to the desert, not wanting him to see the tears escaping her eyes.

"Paige, I know what you're thinking. I want more, too. I want you in a way I haven't been able to have a woman. *Ever.*"

He turned her round to face him. "Do you understand what I'm saying? I want you with my heart, my mind, my body *and* my soul. I've never done that before. Not even with Nahla." He lifted her chin. "I am a virgin in that sense, Paige," he whispered. "And I think you might just be, too." His eyes gleamed with emotion in the moonlight. Her warrior had tears of his own. Her heart squeezed tight.

He brought his lips close to hers. "Do you care about me at all?"

Tears streamed faster down her face. She nodded, not trusting herself to speak, half wondering if this was just one of his seduction techniques.

"Then," he whispered over her mouth, "it could be a first for both of us." He allowed his lips to feather hers, and her legs went limp. "Maybe you could guide me a little," he murmured.

That did it. Heat speared through her belly, snapping her control, melting her fears, blinding all thought. She reached up and threaded her fingers into his thick hair, pulled him down to her, hard, her mouth finding his.

His lips pressed over hers, his energy unleashing, furious, ravaging, his tongue searching, thrusting deep. It made her ache desperately for more. She leaned her body into his, her hands moving up the strong column of his neck. He groaned, his tongue thrusting deeper as he lifted her skirt, his hand finding her thighs, stroking the insides, his calloused fingers rasping against her tender skin. She moved against him, needing him. All of him.

He found her panties, pulled them roughly aside. Her head swam. "Rafiq…I want…"

He kissed her harder, his tongue aggressively silencing her, melting her.

She moved her leg to give him access, felt his hand hot against her wetness, his palm rough, his fingers searching, slipping. She moaned, leaned onto him, tasting the salt of his mouth as beard stubble rasped hard against her cheeks.

His palm rubbed against her, hard. Her insides coiled like a spring, vibrating energy through her, explosive, breathless. She thought of the armies coming, of dawn, the bombs…so little time. He drew her down to the ground, lifted her skirt up above her hips, parted her thighs to the moonlight. She was hot. Wet. Ready. More ready than she'd ever been in her life.

And she knew she—they—might never live to do this again. They might not make it through the mountains. He might not survive a battle with Sadiq. And even if she did lose him, even if she did die, she'd have had something worth living for… She arched her back and lifted herself to him, and she felt him enter her. Thick. Hot. He took her on those crumbling castle walls—a warrior, rhythmically driving into her, an act as old as time.

And no less urgent…as the clock ticked against them.

Chapter 12

Rafiq opened her pale thighs and sank himself into her slick heat, driving himself higher and higher, her skin smooth against his hips, heating under his friction, until the delirium of sweet hot pain shattered through him in violent release.

His fingers dug hard into her back as he shuddered into her. She bucked under him and cried out—one low scream into the desert night as her body dissolved into a ripple of hot contractions around him. The sound of her cry flushed an owl out of the crumbling turrets up high. It fluttered above them, the shadow of its wingspan crossing the moon as it swooped down to the plains in search of prey.

They lay there, atop the stone wall, staring at the sky, fingers laced, utterly content. Words were not possible, and they were not needed. They were too simple a form of communication at a time like this that felt so oddly profound to Rafiq. He'd never felt more complete than at this moment, with this woman lying in his arms. And never more ready to complete what he had to do.

He studied the stars, feeling her body rise and fall against his as she breathed. Dawn would be leaking into the sky soon, and their moment would be broken. Would they ever have one like it again?

The notion of the future hung over him, heavy and ripe with both promise and threat. He closed his eyes, breathed a sigh.

"We must go, Paige."

She nodded.

Rafiq saddled the camels while she rolled up the blankets and filled the goatskin water bags. He placed his hand on her shoulder. "You sure you're ready?"

She stilled, looked up into his eyes. "As ready as I'll ever be." She glanced at the camels, then back at him. "Let's go finish this, shall we?"

He grinned, took her hand. And he knew from that moment they were a unit. They'd shared the deepest of bonds, and whatever happened, that tie would strengthen them on the road ahead. But it would be a dangerous road, and a long one. He hoped the bond would hold.

She lifted the swollen goatskins, carried them over to the camels. Rafiq watched her—the way her hair rippled over her shoulders, the way her skirt swished around her ankles making the bells chink. And a claw suddenly clutched his heart. What he had just gained, he also stood to lose.

He felt his jaw grit and a slow burn ignite down low in

his stomach. *He loved again.* And with the blossoming of that realization inside him, came the rawness of soul that Rafiq knew made him dangerous.

God help anyone who stood in his way this time.

In the crisp dark hours of the dawn, they left the castle walls and began to climb the arduous trail—two spectral black-robed figures on camels—quietly picking their way through sharp rock and dry soil, leaving the ruins far below them.

The sun started to rise over the Empty Quarter, behind the mountains, etching the peaks into a ragged line against the brightening sky. The air grew hot.

Paige's mouth turned dry. Her back began to ache. They were entering a precipitous patch where the stones were small and loose, and each step her camel took sent a small avalanche skittering down into the crevices. One slip, and she'd be gone.

She tried not to look down, to focus instead on Rafiq's solid form. But it didn't quell her growing anxiety as they got higher and the path grew narrower. She held the braided reins tighter, her body growing more and more tense until she was feeling something akin to immobilizing panic.

She stopped the camel in an effort to regain her composure. She knew that half the battle when it came to doing things like this was in the mind. She concentrated on trying to breathe.

Rafiq halted ahead of her. "What's up? You okay?"

She nodded, her mouth dry as the pale sand she was sending down the mountain.

"You sure?"

"I...I'm fine. I just lost my nerve there for a minute."

He waited, patient, until she lifted the reins, nudged the camel, and began to move again. "Talk to me while you ride," he said. "It'll help take your mind off the drop. No one to hear us for miles up here."

She laughed nervously, trying not to look down. "What do you want me to talk about?"

"I don't know…your parents, maybe? You haven't told me what it was like to grow up like that, you know, never going to a proper school, living in the jungle."

He was doing his best, but she really didn't want to talk about her parents. Her parents made her think about loss in relation to love…about the possibility of losing Rafiq. Because she *would* lose him. Even as she thought about it now, she knew a future with him could not be possible. Or was she subconsciously shutting out that possibility because of her past, her fear of abandonment? Here she was self-analyzing again, shutting down emotionally again. Because she was afraid.

She was afraid to let go of that last little nail grip she had on herself and let herself tumble freely down into love.

"Tell me about the Congo," he called over his shoulder.

"And *that's* supposed to make me feel good?"

"Maybe you need to talk, too, Paige. Maybe I also want to know you better."

She swallowed, taking her mind back seventeen years, to the time she was fifteen…to sitting in a huge tent, the air thick as warm soup, bugs bumping on the canvas and mosquito netting. She was doing her homework and it was going to be dark soon, the sudden dark that fell like a black curtain in the jungle so near the equator.

Paige gripped the reins tighter, took her mind further back, to the big fight. It was a memory that stuck out in her mind because she'd never heard her parents yell at each other like that—as if their lives were at stake if they did not get their respective points across.

Her heart blipped. *They had been at stake.* She could see it now that her memory had context after what Rafiq had said about Nexus, Science Reach…Dr. Meyer. Paige ran through the sequence again, rewinding and replaying it like an old movie in her head. Her heart beat faster.

"You still with me, Paige? You okay?"

"I…yes…I was just remembering the fight my parents had before my father left for Brussels to see Dr. Meyer."

"And?"

"It never had context for me before. It was just a bunch of yelling that scared the pants off me because my parents never went at each other like that."

"Do you remember anything about what they were saying?"

"My mother was screaming at my father that his work didn't belong to him. I had no idea what that was about, but I'm guessing now that he'd told her he wanted to defect from Science Reach, and publicize his work for proper peer review. I always thought she was furious…but now that I think about it, I believe she might have been really terrified. My dad was yelling that if he put the word out, *nothing* could happen to them, because the whole world would know."

Paige rocked on her camel, the movements becoming smoother, more hypnotic as the path widened a little. "I guess he didn't listen to her. I guess that's why she was so upset about his trip to Brussels," she said more to herself than him.

She lifted her chin. "I suppose it should encourage me that he had a conscience. But where does that leave my mother?"

"Protective. Like a mother should be. Probably worried about you."

She smiled. He continued to surprise her. He made her feel good about herself.

"How did your parents meet, anyway?" he asked.

"They met in Manhattan. My father was there for a bio-chemical conference, and my mom was apparently in town doing a consulting job for an organization called the Venturion Corporation. It's like a—"

He halted his camel sharply, spun round. "I *know* what it is. It's a high-powered think tank, a nonprofit institution supposedly designed to improve policy and decision-making through research and analysis."

"Yes, it's—"

"Paige," he said, his eyes flashing hotly, "the Venturion Corporation counts top U.S. decision-makers as its clients. It funds high-powered political campaigns, helps shape U.S. policy. *This* could conceivably be the heart of the Cabal." He got his phone out of his saddlebag, quickly punched in a number.

"Sauvage," he barked. "I've got an idea. Get the guys to check out the Venturion Corporation. See if you can find *any* links to Science Reach International, Nexus, BioMed—throw it all in the bag. Dr. Sterling's mother did work for Venturion in Manhattan before—" He threw Paige a questioning glance.

"Before she was given a research grant from Science Reach International, along with my father."

"—before the Sterlings were snapped up by Science Reach and sent into the jungle."

He signed off, pocketed his phone. "I think we might just be on to something."

Paige stared at him. She didn't share his excitement. She felt profoundly unsure about how she *should* feel. These were her parents he was talking about. This was her intimate past. Their mysterious disappearance in that jungle shaped the scientist—the woman—she had become. She had tailored her entire life around searching for answers.

And now that she was finally finding them, it was more unsettling than satisfying. It left her feeling stripped, her foundations gone. The most solid thing in her world right now was that man on his camel. And he didn't belong to her.

He belonged to a nation.

For the first time, she wished he didn't have to come back to Hamān. And she felt sick with selfishness because of it.

They rounded a ridge as the sun exploded over the mountains in a crashing symphony of color that caused the landscape to burst into life. Shades of deep purple and gray rippled into nuances of ochre and dusty olive-green. Heat swelled instantly with the color, chasing heavier, cooler currents of air down to hide in deep, dark crevices.

Paige caught her breath. It was as if some great giant had turned on the lights and fired the furnace. They rounded the next curve and Rafiq stopped. Spilling down the hillside in front of them was a tightly terraced patchwork of farmland. A path zigzagged between the pockets of land to a small stone house. A wisp of smoke curled up from the chimney.

"I can't believe people actually live up here. How do they manage to farm this stuff?"

"It's a hard life," said Rafiq, studying the vista. "These

mountain dwellers are a unique and tough breed. Many are exiles from a more mainstream life."

"I guess by hiding out in the mountains they can avoid Sadiq's iron hand."

He studied her, a strange look in his eyes. He opened his mouth to say something, then thought better of it, turned away, and nudged his camel on.

Paige felt suddenly abandoned. She tried to shake the sensation, telling herself she was just tired. But it lingered like the cold air down in the crevices, hidden from the sun's warmth.

The sun was white-hot and at its zenith when they heard a helicopter in the mountains for the third time. The Royal Hamānian Air Force had joined the hunt. The first two helicopters had flown farther to the northeast, scanning the route through the saddle, where they'd originally planned to travel. This chopper was closer. They were broadening their search, circling out from the saddle.

Rafiq raised his binoculars, scanned the hazy peaks for a sign of the helo. He figured he and Paige were at an elevation of around eight thousand two hundred feet now. The height and terrain and the midday glare of the sun would not be making it easy for the pilot. Then he saw the chopper, the size of a black gnat in his scopes. It grew rapidly in size, taking discernible form. This one was heading right their way.

"Quick, we need to dismount." He couched the camels with a sharp cluck of his tongue.

The sound of the beating blades swelled into the gorge as the pilot found the trail they were on and began to follow its course.

"Run, Paige," he yelled as she slid from the saddle. He grabbed the ropes. "Get under that rock ledge up there!"

Stones clattered down the mountain as she lifted her skirt and scrambled up the trail. He trotted after her, jerking the beasts behind him. They balked, growing more and more edgy and obstreperous as the sound of the chopper grew louder.

Rafiq coaxed the camels under the overhang, squeezed himself in beside Paige, pulled the animals closer, using their sandy color as a shield. It was hot. The animals' breath was heavy. He could smell the warm rock.

Paige's eyes were wide in the slit of her *chador* and as the helicopter neared, they remained steadily fixed on him.

He slipped his arm around her, held her tight. He could feel her heart beat against his chest.

The chopper hovered somewhere above them, then the machine began to lower slowly into the valley. The pilot must have seen something, decided to come down for a closer look.

Waves of sound thudded into their shallow cave and beat deafeningly against their eardrums. The helicopter came lower and lower, stirring sand into a blinding blizzard. The camels jerked sharply, yanking the rope against their nose rings. Rafiq held them firmly, he pulled Paige's head down against his chest, he tucked his chin into his neck and scrunched his eyes shut against the stinging sand.

The chopper came lower still. Rafiq squinted sideways through the gap in his turban. He could see the skids. A few more inches and the pilot or his spotter would see them. He felt for Paige's hand, pushed the camel ropes into her palm, wrapped her fingers over them, and squeezed, showing her that she had to hang on. He lifted his tunic, reached for his firearm. He slid it out of his holster, and held it ready.

The chopper inched even lower. Rafiq fingered the trigger softly. He didn't want to have to use the weapon. A downed chopper would pinpoint their location in seconds—via radio, smoke, explosion. They would never make it to the border.

It hovered, moved slightly to the left, then back in front of their hide, then suddenly it veered up and lifted back up into the sky.

Breath punched out of him. He blinked against the grit in his lashes, slipped his gun back into the holster and waited for the dust to settle. The clapping sound died gradually into the hills to the west, and his muscles eased.

"Thank God," she whispered.

He looked into her kohl-rimmed eyes and the intensity there speared him in the gut.

"Rafiq," she whispered.

"What is it?"

"Will…will you just hold me a second, please?"

Emotion rushed through him. He drew her tightly into himself, held her hard against his body, feeling her beating heart. "It'll be okay, Paige."

"How do you know?"

He frowned. She hadn't been like this when he'd kidnapped her. She'd been resolute, even in her fear. Now that spark of independent defiance seemed to be missing. Was she also afraid of what tomorrow might hold? Could she possibly care enough about him to be worried she'd lose him? Rafiq's heart began to burn. He held her even tighter.

"I know it'll be okay, Paige," he whispered, "because I *believe* it will."

* * *

14:00 Charlie, Venturion Tower, Manhattan, Saturday,
October 4

Black clouds swallowed the dawn skyline. Rain continued to click against the windows. He hadn't slept at all, and
for the first time in decades, razor teeth of anxiety bit hard
into his usual steel calm.

The constant sound of the metronome from his antique
grandfather clock was driving his anxiety deeper. It was
already Saturday afternoon in Hamān. When was his man
going to call? How much longer could he give him?

He needed to meet with the others as soon as possible.
But what to tell them? No one knew about his personal
assassin. Knowledge of the murders he'd commissioned in
the past would be ammunition against him.

The door swung open behind him, slicing light into the
dark room. He jumped and spun round.

"Dad? I didn't mean to startle you. Are you all right?"

"Olivia, darling." His pulse slowed to an acceptable
pace. He held his arms open, stepped forward to embrace
his daughter. "I'm fine. Just…planning my day."

"In the dark?" She reached over, flicked on a lamp.

"I think better in the dark. What are you doing here at
this hour?"

"I wanted to pick up those policy papers before I fly out
to Washington." She checked her watch. "And I've got to
run. My plane leaves in less than an hour." She pecked him
on the cheek.

He cocked a brow and grinned. "Seeing Forbes for
dinner tonight?"

She hesitated. "No…I'm lunching with him tomorrow."

"Excellent."

"It's social, Dad. There's nothing…serious between me and Grayson."

Irritation twinged through him, but he showed no outward sign. He never did. Not to his daughter.

"He's the world's most eligible bachelor. And you—" he skimmed her jaw with the back of his hand "—you're one hell of a catch, darling, even for the vice president. You're right for him, and he knows it."

You're destined for the White House, Olivia. You will be first lady of the most powerful country on earth, once we're done. The world will be at our feet.

Olivia frowned. Something was bothering her father. The rest of the world might not be able to read him, but she could. And this subtle undercurrent she detected in him…it touched her with an eerie sense of déjà vu. It reminded her of another time he'd had that edgy look in his eyes.

Olivia's skin went cold as her mind dragged her involuntarily back to when she was nineteen years old, to the night she'd told her father that she was going to marry Jack Sauer.

The night before the murder.

14:22 Charlie, Asir Mountains, Saturday, October 4

It was late afternoon by the time Paige and Rafiq began to traverse a high plateau, slowly making their way southeast.

And it came out of the blue, exploded over a rock ridge and barreled toward them in a blur of snarling gray fur.

A wild dog.

Paige's brain didn't have time to register it before the beast flashed its teeth, gave a bloodcurdling howl and lunged at her camel's legs.

The camel lurched, screamed like a banshee, kicked,

swung its serpentine neck round and sank its yellowed incisors into the dog's neck.

Paige was flung sideways in the saddle as she dropped the reins in a desperate bid to hang on to the kicking, spitting beast.

The camel kicked again, hard.

The dog went flying, rolled in a yelping blur, as Paige lost her grip and thudded to the ground, air whooshing out of her lungs in an explosion of pain.

She scrambled to her feet instantly, thinking the dog was going to come at her, tear her throat.

But it was shrieking in unearthly pain as it scampered back toward the ridge, red blood on the mottled grey fur at its neck. It collapsed in front of a rock.

Paige tried to catch her breath. She was shaking. Rafiq was at her side, scimitar unsheathed, watching the ridge as if expecting another wild cur to barrel over and come at them. Then she heard why. A faint chorus of yipping grew louder and louder—*a whole pack of dogs.*

Her eyes flashed to his in terror. "It's okay." He stayed her with his hand, pointed his scimitar at the ridge. "Watch."

A dusty brown figure, a man who looked as if he'd been sculpted out of the dry earth itself, materialized over the ridge, leading a horse and two mules. He was surrounded by a pack of dogs.

The man saw them, and stopped. He studied them from the distance, then dismounted from his horse. He bent down and scooped the wounded animal into his arms. He carried it over to his horse, and deftly lifted himself and his dog into the saddle. He took his reins in hand, cradling the wounded animal in his lap, the others milling quietly about his feet.

Paige stared in shock.

Only then did the man lift his head and look at them again. His dust-caked and leathered face was expressionless under his tattered dun turban. His shoes were old leather but his sword, knife and rifle looked newer. He made no move to touch his weapons.

"Mountain hunter," Rafiq whispered. "They use both wild and domestic dogs. They go after the Asir leopard, and anything else they can find. See the hares and the hyena strapped to the mules behind him?"

She nodded. But it was the man's face that snared her attention. The hunter's wordless, expressionless stare seemed to be working its way right into her soul. And she found herself feeling sorry about his dog.

The hunter turned his attention back to his animal. He began to manipulate its leg, then its fur, assessing the extent of injury. The dog didn't make a sound. It was either badly hurt, or it trusted its master implicitly.

"I...it just came for me," Paige called out in Arabic. "My camel—"

"*Shut up!*" Rafiq hissed, his eyes hot with warning.

She glared at him, angry at herself for having spoken, for having needed to say something to the man with the injured animal.

The hunter edged his mount forward, studied her closely, but said nothing. Then he looked sharply, directly, at Rafiq.

Rafiq raised his hand in a salute of greeting.

The man bowed his head suddenly. He sat like that for a long moment. Reverent. Then he turned his horse, continued along his path, his pack of dogs mobilizing, yipping behind him.

They watched until he disappeared through the rocks and the sound of his dogs died into the wind.

Paige realized her heart was thumping hard, that her hip hurt. She began to wonder if what had just happened had been real.

"You shouldn't have opened your mouth," he snapped. "You speak damn fine Arabic but you still have an accent, *especially* in these parts."

"I'm sorry. I...I couldn't help it. His dog was hurt."

"Wasn't your fault!"

"I...I know, but...there was something about him. Something...kind."

Rafiq's eyes softened. "It's okay. Your speaking probably makes no difference, anyway. We stand out a mile around here no matter what."

"Will he report us?"

"That man—" said Rafiq, gazing at the gap in the rocks where he'd disappeared "—he saw nothing."

"He looked as if...as if he might have recognized you. Do you think word has spread this far, already?"

Rafiq nodded slowly. "He knew who I was." He turned to her. "But men like him, they keep secrets, Paige."

She stared at the rocks where he'd disappeared. *What if he didn't?* She shivered suddenly with a chilling sense of foreboding.

Chapter 13

The hunter could sense danger in the long evening shadows before he even saw his small stone house. He placed his hand on the fur of his injured dog, rode slowly forward. His wife and children were waiting for him.

When he saw no smoke rising from the chimney, he *knew* something was wrong.

The soldiers materialized like ghosts out of the twilight, rifles trained on him.

They wanted to know what had happened to his dog, who he'd seen up in the peaks.

He said nothing.

They forced him to dismount, jabbed muzzles into his thin ribs, cracked a rifle butt across his face. Blood ran warm down his cheek.

He insisted he had seen no one.

They pushed him through the door of his own home...and his heart stilled.

A man—a ghost-man with colorless eyes—stood holding the blade of a scimitar across his daughter's neck. The hair on the back of the hunter's neck rose. His body could tell evil.

His eyes adjusted to the dimness in his home and he saw his wife and son bound and gagged in the corner, pushed up against the stone wall. His wife's face was sheened with tears, her eyes huge and frightened.

The ghost-man said something, and a soldier translated. "Tell us who you saw in the mountains or we will slit your daughter's throat."

The hunter swallowed. "I saw no one. What makes you think I saw anyone?"

"Who hurt your dog?"

"It was a baboon," he said, looking into his daughter's eyes, wondering how much he must pay to protect the sultan he'd seen in the hills...how much he must pay to save Hamān.

"You are lying, old man."

He shook his head. "I saw no one," he said softly, unable to betray the king, the promise of a future for his people.

The ghost moved his hand, pressing the blade into his daughter's neck. She gasped. Her eyes went wide, pleading for help.

"*Wait!* I did see someone."

"Who!" barked the soldier in charge.

"A man and a woman, traveling on camels."

The ghost-man said something. The soldier turned sharply to the hunter. "That man and his woman are fugitives. We have lost their tracks. You will use your dogs. You *will* find them. And then your family will live."

The big ghost flung his daughter to the side. She sank to the floor in a sobbing heap. His son stood silent and brave. His wife's eyes held his.

He prayed that God and his country would forgive him for what he was being forced to do.

18:05 Charlie, Asir Mountains, Saturday, October 4

Clouds rolled over the peaks, swallowing the trail with curtains of hot mist. This region of the Asir was subject to Indian Ocean monsoons October through March. This looked like the first of them.

Paige was beyond exhausted, and her mind kept wandering, seeing shapes in the mist.

A wolf howled somewhere in the grayness.

She shuddered in spite of the heat. The sound was eerie, distorted through the swirling layers. It was getting darker, visibility becoming even more challenging. The *chador* didn't help. Rafiq was now just a shape in the fog ahead of her. If she lost sight of him, she'd be lost for good.

He was right; she'd never have made it over here alone.

Then just as the mist swallowed him completely, she saw them—gathered along the ridge, dark forms watching their progress. Her heart stalled.

She halted her camel, spun round in the saddle. There were more, on the opposite ridge, fading in and out of the mist.

They were surrounded!

Her heart began to jackhammer. "Rafiq!"

He materialized out of the mists. *"What?"*

"Look!" she whispered. "Up there on the ridge."

He turned slowly. Stilled. Then he threw back his head and laughed loud.

Confusion spiraled through Paige. "What—"

"Paige, sweetheart, I thought you of all people would recognize a troop of wild primates." He leaned forward in his saddle. "Those are baboons. They've been following us for a while now."

"Oh," she whispered. She looked back up at the blurry dark shapes that surrounded them. "I can't believe I did that…I can't…I…" Emotion swamped her. She blinked it back. She was so tired, and her mind so confused she'd thought they were soldiers. And now she really was frightened, because she'd lost her mind, the one thing she relied upon most.

She turned to Rafiq in desperation.

He squeezed her arm. "Happens to the best of us."

"No, it doesn't!" she snapped. "They're Hamadryas baboons. Indigenous to Arabia. I should have recognized that's what was up there. They have one of the most highly structured social systems among primates," she said, trying prove to Rafiq she was not a total jackass, that she was not *totally* dependent on him. But it was a lie. She was.

And now it was worse. Because she'd fallen for him, and she didn't want to lose him. And that fear was burrowing deep into her soul in a way she couldn't control. It was beginning to consume her. She kept trying to fight it off, telling herself it was fatigue. But it wouldn't go away.

She somehow had to stop it. She *had* to pull herself together. She needed to block herself to all this emotion.

To him.

Before she did something really stupid, dangerous.

* * *

18:30 Charlie, FDS base, São Diogo Island, Saturday, October 4

December Ngomo seated himself in the leather chair in front of Sauvage's desk. He wiggled a fat file of papers in the air. "Zayed was right—the Venturion Corporation is linked to Nexus, Science Reach *and* BioMed. It's the common denominator." He slapped the dossier onto Sauvage's desk with a broad smile. "Check it out, *mon ami*, there's more. Lots more. These guys, this board of directors—" he jabbed his index finger on the dossier "—*are* the Cabal, I'd stake my life on it. I've got our techs digging into the history of each and every one of those Venturion board members. By the time we're done, we'll know who was toilet trained by whom and when. I guarantee it."

Sauvage reached for the file, drew it across his desk toward himself. "Who is head of the Venturion board?"

"Samuel Killinger, photos are at the back."

Sauvage froze.

He felt the blood drain from his head.

He said nothing as he opened the file, shuffled quickly through to the back, slid out a set of black-and-white glossies.

He stared at the photo on top, and his throat closed. "Where is this one from?" His voice came out hoarse.

December frowned, leaned forward. "Got that one off the news wires. That—" he pointed to the image "—is Samuel Killinger with his daughter—"

"*Olivia.*"

December glanced up. "You *know* her?"

Sauvage concentrated on his breathing. Steady. Slow. In. Out. "Once. In another life."

December nodded slowly, his eyes searching Sauvage's

face. But he said nothing. They never talked about the past—ever. Each of them had things to hide. Serious things.

Sauvage flipped over to the next photo and his gut clenched.

"That," said December, "is Olivia Killinger with Vice President Grayson Forbes."

Sauvage closed his eyes. His head swam. He couldn't breathe, goddammit.

"Forbes is dating her. If the Cabal wins this one, Olivia Killinger looks set to be the first lady."

Sauvage slammed his fist on the desk and jerked to his feet. This mission had just taken on a whole new meaning.

20:01 Charlie, Asir Mountains, Saturday, October 4

The first few drops shot like bullets from the sky, and within seconds, the rain was a lashing curtain, and darkness was complete.

Rafiq realized they'd have to stop. It was getting treacherously slippery along the narrowing plateau. From the topo maps he'd memorized, the plateau would squeeze into a rocky bridge between the peaks and then fork out into two trails—one that led to the southwest, and another that circumnavigated wadi Bi'sash, a large body of water trapped by an underlying lava bed.

The route via the wadi opened out onto a ridge overlooking the southern flanks of the Asir. Beyond it, the Yemeni plateau stretched to the Gulf of Aden. That's the way they had to go.

He pushed his sodden turban back off his head. It was pouring water into his eyes. Blinking into the rain, he took the camel rope from Paige and yoked her animal to his.

"You just have to hang on until we can find a place to hole up until the worst of this monsoon blows itself out," he yelled into the storm.

He leaned into the sheet of rain and pressed on, searching for shelter among the rocks.

Then he heard it again—a faint yip carried on the wind, so distant he almost wondered if he'd imagined it. But then there was another snatch of sound. And another. Rafiq slowed, trying to ascertain the direction from which the sounds came. For a while he heard nothing more.

They rounded a ridge of rock, and the wind abated for a second. Immediately he heard the distant yelping.

He tensed. *Hunting dogs!*

No hunter with half a brain cell would be out in this weather. That could mean only one thing. Someone was hunting *them*.

He stopped the camels, pulled Paige's animal up close so that she could hear him over the storm. "I think they're using dogs to come after us," he yelled into the rain. "Sounds like they've picked up our trail. If that hunter we saw this morning told the military, whoever is coming for us is going to be well armed, and we're going to be outnumbered. The only option we have is to try and outrun them, and pray this weather destroys our tracks. Trust your camel, okay, Paige? Just stay behind me. And hang on."

"You said the hunter wouldn't talk," she shouted into the wind.

"Maybe he had no choice." He leaned over his animal, pressed the hilt of his *jambiya* into her hand. "Take this."

She resisted,

"Take it, Paige!"

Rafiq said a silent prayer to the powers of nature. It was

something he hadn't done in decades. But he needed the rain to keep coming hard, to cover their scent. He was no match against a pack of wild hunting dogs. Blind faith and sure-footed camels were going to have to pull them through these next few hours.

"Yaaaah!" He kicked his camel, showing his urgency. And the beast responded. He bent low into the wind and rain. The path ahead growing narrower, more rocky. The chorus of yipping in the distance behind them swelled until it braided into the howling wind.

The pack was closing in.

Rafiq's heart beat faster. He kicked his animal to a full run, knowing that one slip would send them *all* flailing down either side of this narrow bridge between peaks.

He could feel Paige's camel yawing from side to side as it was tugged behind his. "Hang on, Doctor," he whispered to himself. "Just hang the hell on."

The ground began to slope sharply downward and his camel's body began to rock wildly from side to side. Camels didn't do downhill well. Their legs moved in concert, and they tended to break into an uncontrollable, seesawing run, gathering speed with the incline.

Rafiq tried to rein his animal in a little, but it barreled maniacally down into blackness. Rafiq could see nothing, but he could sense the ground falling dangerously away on either side of their small caravan. He could feel the hollow emptiness of dark space beside them.

And he could hear the dogs clearly now, along with snatches of male voices, shouting. His heart pounded in his throat. He'd hoped the rain would have destroyed their trail, but these mountain dogs were uncanny trackers—and killers—once they got the scent. He and Paige weren't going to make it…

His camel stumbled suddenly and balked to an abrupt halt.

Rafiq lurched forward in the saddle. "Yaaah!" He kicked at his animal, but it wouldn't budge. Then he realized why. *Water!* They'd reached wadi Bi'sash.

Thank you, God.

Only trouble was, his camel didn't appear to be a swimmer. Rafiq stroked the animal's neck, whispered in soft Arabic, coaxing with his voice, nudging with his heels.

Behind them the chorus of the dogs drew louder. He could hear men's voices clearly.

He nudged again, straining against his urgency to be gentle with his mount. And finally the camel moved, the sound of water beginning to slosh about its knees. Paige's camel followed without protest.

Rafiq let go of the air he'd been holding in his chest.

"We've reached the wadi," he called out in a hushed voice. "If we can wade through it, we can lose the dogs. The mist will hide us."

"Is it deep?"

"It's fine," he lied. He had no idea how deep the water was, but it was their *only* chance.

He pulled Paige and her camel in behind him…deeper, and deeper. He kept going until the water lapped warm against his thighs. Any deeper and the camel was going to lose footing and have to swim. He wasn't sure if it would hold their weight, the weight of the supplies, and stay afloat.

He heard the dogs yelping madly along the shoreline. One howled like a wolf into the wind. A man yelled. Then another screamed. They were angry, fighting amongst each other. A shot was fired. Then another.

God, he hoped the soldiers weren't taking this out on the hunter. Rafiq could only imagine what they might have done to make him cooperate—and what they'd do to him if he failed. And he just had.

Rafiq vowed that if he ever made it back into Hamān alive, he would find that man's family and do what he could to put things right.

But if they'd killed the hunter, the soldiers were short-sighted fools. They'd have no control over the dogs, no way of picking up their scent again later in the night. He and Paige would be safe for a while—at least until morning, if they could find some place to hide and rest.

A bullet splashed into the lake beside him. Then another, falling just short of his camel's flanks. The men were firing blindly over the wadi. Rafiq swore softly, urged his mount a little faster, but moving him to the left this time, hoping to find shallower water. His camel found higher footing. Relief flooded through him.

Rafiq worked his camel so that every time he felt it go deeper, he'd coax the animal farther to the left, back into shallows. He figured he was working his way parallel to the shoreline by doing this.

He kept checking back, but Paige wasn't making a sound behind her. She was hanging onto that camel in stoic silence. He swiped water from his eyes. He had to admire that control. He admired a hell of a lot about this woman.

Lightning cracked and he jerked in his saddle. The simultaneous explosion of light and sound meant the storm was right over them.

His camel slipped, staggered and regained balance. The lake bed was growing silty, the water getting shallower. They'd made it across.

He concentrated on navigating the animals over the boggy ground toward firmer land. They couldn't afford a fall now, or to injure an animal. The camels were tired enough as it was. They all needed rest if they were to try and make a run for the Yemeni border at first light.

Another flash of light split the sky. Rafiq blinked sharply as the world flickered white, then black. The next crack of thunder followed a bit later, rolling into the distant peaks. The storm was moving on.

But in that flash he'd seen something—a black hole in rock, a cave entrance. Excitement nipped at him.

He guided the camels toward it, moving by memory.

Another flash illuminated the landscape for a nanosecond, and he saw they'd reached it. He halted the camels, couched them and dismounted.

"Wait here."

He found the cave and fingered his way along the entrance, loath to use his flashlight lest the soldiers see it from across the lake. The inside was warm and the air smelled dry. The ground was dry, too, mostly sand and some small rocks and stones.

He paused, listening for the sounds of any animal that may be holed up in the cave. He could hear—and sense—nothing.

He flicked his flashlight on once he was deeper inside, and shadows leaped around the small halo. The cave was so vast he could not see the back of it. He lit a small emergency flare, tossed it into the depths of the cave. The entire enclosure exploded in stark pink-white relief.

There were no wild eyes watching him, but there were signs of a small kill, maybe a rabbit. He toed the remains. It had probably been dinner for a caracul—a wildcat indigenous to the region. But it was gone now. There were also twigs and dry branches, probably left by some nomadic traveler who'd stopped here for the night. His heart lifted. It was perfect.

He could feed and water the camels here, and Paige could get some sleep. With luck, the soldiers and dogs would retreat and be long gone by morning.

Rafiq led Paige and the camels into their new shelter. She removed her sodden *chador* and was as white as porcelain in the gleam of his flashlight, her eyes big and dark. She was in shock. He quickly untied the waterproof saddlebags and hobbled the camels at the entrance, using their bodies to block any light from the small fire he planned to build near the back of the cave. The camels would also ward off any wild animals that planned to return during the night, and hopefully alert him to any human approach.

He dragged the saddlebags into the cave, set his handgun on a rock, and made sure his scimitar was within easy reach. His dagger he'd given to Paige, and in the morning, he'd make sure she knew how best to use it.

He unpacked the bags, looking for a tarp, and was pleasantly surprised to find the carpet dealer had managed to include one, along with an assault rifle in two parts. He set the weapon aside and laid the tarp out on the soft dry sandy part of the cave. He told Paige that if she stripped out of her sodden skirt and blouse he could try and dry her clothes a little before sunrise.

He handed her a blanket to use as cover, along with a foil packet of military-style rations.

She undressed while he built a fire using the dry wood. As soon as it caught, he shed his wet tunic and T-shirt. He draped them over a rock near the flames next to her clothes, and he turned to Paige.

She was sitting on the tarp, her body turned to the warmth of the flames, knees pulled up against her breasts, the blanket draped loosely over her back. Rafiq tried to keep his gaze confined to her eyes, not on skin that glowed like gold-brushed porcelain in the flickering light of flames. He tried not to obsess with the fact her panties were jet-black lace and matched her bra. He hadn't noticed that in the dim light on the parapet, lost in the heat of passion. He swallowed, unable to avoid the sudden image of black lace under a clinical white lab coat, or the swell of her breasts hidden in a hazmat suit. He felt himself go hard and hot.

And angry. She was a loner, he could see that now. And vulnerable. That was what had made her so attractive to the Cabal, apart from her mental prowess. They had abused her personality, shaped her from the day of her parents' death, for their own evil purpose.

It made his blood boil. If he ever got his hands on—

"Rafiq?"

He shook himself. He knelt down in front of her, worry brushing over him. "What is it, Paige?" he asked.

She leaned forward, her kohl-lined eyes intense, mysterious. "I need you," she said in a whisper that sent nerves shivering over his skin.

No one had said that to him. Not in *that* way. And he understood. He felt it, too. His heart began to thud, his breathing became ragged.

But he held back. She was vulnerable right now. He couldn't...

She let the blanket slip down off her back, and she unclasped her bra, allowing it to drop. Her nipples were dusky rose in color. A small bead of water escaped a wet strand of her hair, rolled down the swell of her breast and dangled from the end of her nipple, catching the reflection of the fire like a jewel.

Blood drained from his head, and his groin began to pulse with heat. He stared, mesmerized by the glittering drop of water. He closed his eyes for a second, trying to remember where he was, who she was, why they were here in this cave. Why he was back in Hamān. But it was all gone. Nothing existed apart from this moment. There was only Paige.

She reached out, threaded her fingers through his damp hair and drew him down toward her. Rafiq moved his mouth toward her breast, toward the drop of water, and he sucked it in softly, the inside seam of his lips just teasing her nipple. It hardened instantly under his mouth and she moaned softly, drawing his head more firmly to her breast.

He circled her nipple with a quick flick of his tongue as he ran his hand along the inside of her thigh until he felt the roughness of lace. He cupped her mound. She was hot, damp.

She moved her ankles further apart, opening access, her heat radiating out from her against his palm.

He grew so hard he felt like he might explode just touching her.

He moved his hands around her hips, began to pull her panties down. He was breathing hard. She lifted her hips as he peeled her underwear off, and dizziness spiraled through him at the sight of her. He sat back, undid his pants, took them off, his eyes holding hers as he did.

He knelt back down in front of her, placed his hands on her knees, pushing her open wider, exposing her to the flickering glow of the flames.

Chapter 14

He knelt between her legs. Firelight danced over his body, shifting shadows. She trailed her eyes down his chest, over his rippling abdomen. Down to his arousal.

Her breath lodged in her throat.

With a hand on each of her knees, he forced her open wide. She could feel the warmth of the flames against her, and she felt herself begin to ache with almost unbearable need.

He lowered himself slowly between her legs, his tongue finding her, teasing with small, slick movements. He hit a spot that made her writhe and lift herself to him, and he began to move with soft, longer, caressing, rhythmic strokes, going a little deeper each time until Paige began to shake against her control, until she thought she would scream for release.

But he stopped suddenly, sat back, opened her legs even wider, then leaned over her, covering her with his body and thrust into her sharply. Paige gasped with pleasure. She could feel him inside, hot, almost quivering with intensity. She couldn't restrain herself. She threw her head back, arched up to him, clutching his back, forcing him to go deeper and harder, hungry, her want so raw it cut right into her soul.

He groaned and plunged deeper. Moving harder, rougher, his mouth over hers, his teeth scoring, his tongue slipping until she was driven to a peak that hovered between pain and thrill. And she shattered.

Her release cracked any control he had left. He drove into her with wild abandon as the storm beat outside, water running over the mouth of the cave in a glowing sheen.

And he came in a shuddering explosive release that caused aftershocks to ripple through her like the thunder that was rolling back into the hills.

They lay sated, naked and warm in front of the flames, and Paige knew she'd reached a turning point.

Tonight she'd touched both death and life. She'd climbed up into these mountains and been forced to tread a nebulous line between pain and pleasure, hatred and love.

Fear and trust.

And now, up here in the safety of this cave along the narrow spine of the Asir, she felt as if they were delicately suspended between yesterday and tomorrow. The past and the future.

And she was scared, dammit.

When that storm outside lifted and day broke, it was going to be downhill. They'd make a run for the Yemeni border, and who knew what lay beyond that?

She didn't want to think about tomorrow. She didn't

want to think about anything. Because she liked it right here in this cave, suspended between it all. Right now, she was complete.

She fell asleep in his arms, breathing in his scent, relaxing into the security of his strength, listening to the crack and pop of the fire and the steady drum of rain outside.

Rafiq's heart began to thud hard. This was it—this was the woman he intended to make his queen. If she let him.

He'd make her see that he was the one for her, that she could have everything she needed right here in Hamān, with him. He'd build her a Level 4 lab right inside the palace if that's what it took.

The wind howled outside and a darkening sense of doubt circled. He shoved it away. He would *not* entertain doubt. He would *believe*. He would have faith that—although the road would be long, and lives would be lost—it would lead where he wanted. Home. With her. Here in Hamān.

And when he came back with Paige at his side, his land would be free.

He sucked in a fierce and shuddering breath, and he stroked her hair gently. Yes, he had faith.

When the sky turned pearl gray, Rafiq dragged his damp, smoky T-shirt over his head and pulled his hair back into a thong.

He gathered his weapons and stepped out of the cave. The world was deathly silent—no birds, no wind, nothing. And the air was close and hot, hanging with a thick kind of anticipation.

Or foreboding.

He shook it off immediately and started to prepare the

camels. Once they were saddled, he walked to the edge of the cliff, raised his scopes, and scanned the terrain. Way down in the distance were desert plains that stretched to the Saudi Arabian border in the north and to the Yemeni border in the south. Sadiq's men would expect him to try and cross into Saudi Arabia, because the border into Yemen was closed and hostile.

Yemen had become the archenemy of Hamān since Sadiq had annexed the strip of land that led down to the Gulf of Aden. It was that corridor of sand that would take them down to the coastal estuary. Sauvage would have a fishing boat waiting for them out in the open waters. They needed to be down at that estuary by nightfall. They were still seven thousand feet up, and they were going to have to run a military gauntlet to get there.

He punched Sauvage's number into his phone and called in his ETA. Sauvage assured him the boat would be waiting. December was already in Djibouti and he would accompany the crew. When Rafiq signaled, December would use an inflatable raft and row quietly into the estuary. A chopper would pick Paige up from the fishing vessel once they were clear of the coast and evacuate her to Djibouti, where a fueled jet and pilots were already on standby to fly her in to the FDS base on São Diogo Island. Dr. Meyer and his team were ready and waiting for her in the lab.

This was the endgame.

Rafiq signed off, and he felt her, behind him, watching. He turned slowly.

She stood in the entrance to the cave, her hair loose over her shoulders, a mercurial look in her eyes which right now were the same color as the pearl-gray sky.

"Hey, soldier," she said, smiling softly, taking a step toward him.

Warmth blossomed through him. "Hey, princess."

Her smile faded, a strange pensiveness shifting into her eyes. "I guess I should have said, 'Hey, sultan.'" She paused. "How does one address a sultan the morning after, anyway? Is there a certain protocol, depending on the rank of wife in the harem?" An edge of bitterness had crept into her voice.

"Paige—" he took a step toward her "—that's not fair."

She blinked rapidly, pushed her hair back from her face. "I'm sorry, Rafiq. That was totally uncalled for. I just…I'm so sorry:…I'll get my *chador* and I'll be ready to go." She spun round and disappeared into the cave.

He cursed.

He should never have called her princess. It was a totally dumb thing to have said. It drew attention to his title, to the distance they yet had to travel between them, and now was not the time. They had to focus on keeping their heads clear and getting down to that ocean.

And stopping the Cabal.

But when she came out of the cave with her damp *chador* bundled under her arm and a haunted look in her kohl-smudged eyes, his heart spasmed, and he knew in his gut he had to do—say—*something*.

Paige needed to think positively—about getting out alive. About the future. And above all, he selfishly wanted to be assured that she was thinking positively about *them*. He wanted something that would carry him in her mind through the next hours, days.

He took her hands in his. "Paige," he said, looking deep into her eyes, "I want to set a date with you."

Confusion rippled through her features. "I...I don't understand."

"What are you doing on Tuesday night?"

Her eyes grew grave. "That's in two days."

"That's right."

She closed her eyes, and her features went tight.

A sense of uneasiness, foreboding, whispered through him. "Paige? I want to go on a date with you. I want to see you, properly, once we've gotten out of here."

She couldn't do this. She simply could *not* set a date and a time that would force her to sit and watch the hands of a clock while she waited...and waited...and waited...with the horrific realization growing inside her like a cancer that someone she cared about would not be coming back to her. Ever. Like that night in the Congo—the night that had changed the rest of her life.

She'd stared at the hands on the watch her dad had given her for her fifteenth birthday only three weeks earlier, waiting for her parents to return to camp. They'd gone into the Blacklands after the bonobo troop, and they were late. They'd missed supper. Darkness had fallen. She'd watched the seconds tick past on her watch, and with each miniscule movement of that hand, the fear they were not coming back had burrowed deeper.

She'd sat up like that until dawn leaked into the sky, and still they weren't home. She'd known then that the jungle had swallowed them forever, that she was now completely alone, save for five Congolese porters who spoke no English, in the darkest most unexplored place on the African continent.

When the sun rose and the little hands had moved right

around the face of her watch, four of the guides were gone
with most of the supplies, including the radio.

If it hadn't been for that one man who'd stayed
behind… Paige blinked back her emotion. It had taken the
two of them over two weeks to find civilization and when
she'd come out of that jungle, she'd been thin, sick with
dysentery, covered in leeches and forever changed. She
still had memories of that time she would never speak
about to anyone.

The Science Reach people had been completely shocked
that she'd survived. In retrospect, knowing what Rafiq had
told her, maybe they hadn't intended her to make it.

She didn't like to think about that time, but it had made
her who she was. Independent. A realist. Someone who
wasn't going to wait with hope in her heart.

Hope was a useless commodity. It was better to be
prepared. Just like she'd believed in the Nexus mandate,
that it was better to create the viruses and have the anti-
dotes ready, prepared, before the enemy came at you.

"Paige," he said, his voice going deeper, his hands tightening around hers. "A dinner date, you know? Candles,
music…" His voice faded.

"What if we don't make it, Rafiq?"

"We *will* make it."

"How can you be so sure?"

"Because I've made it out of far, far worse. And I
believe. You have *got* to believe, Paige."

She stared into his eyes. *Believe what? That everything
will just end happily ever after? That I won't be indicted?
That you will come back and take over Hamān without
major incident and be back in time for dinner? Who are
you kidding, Rafiq? Yourself or me?*

"Rafiq…" she chose her words very carefully. "You said you'd return to Hamān."

His brows lowered. "And I will."

"Then how can you make a date? You can't make promises now. *I* can't make promises. *If* you survive a battle with Sadiq, you will have a duty to your people. And I have an antidote to make, a justice system to face, an entire life to put right. Our future—our lives—do not belong to *us* right now."

Ferocity flashed in his eyes. "It's not like I'm asking you to map out your entire life."

"I can't." She pulled her hands free. "I can't make promises I can't keep, and neither should you. I can't sit and wait—"

His mouth flattened into a harsh line. He jerked round, strode over to the camels, began to pack the bags.

—for someone I love to come home.

Her stomach was a ball of pain. Her mouth and throat were dry, and her eyes burned. She watched his muscles ripple under his T-shirt as he hefted the bags onto the camels and secured them to the saddles. *Oh God, what have I just done?*

"Rafiq?" She desperately wanted him to understand— that she would give so much to be with him on that date, to believe that D-day would pass, that the clock would tick quietly past midnight into a new day. And the world would wake, just as it had the day before, oblivious to the narrow escape—that there actually could be a future for them.

"Rafiq!"

He ignored her. He flung his tunic over his head, cinched it at the waist, shoved his scimitar into his belt and wrapped his turban deftly over his face. The man she'd made love to disappeared in front of her eyes, morphing once again into some mysterious and lethal Arabian ninja.

"Rafiq, please, I need you to understand!"

But he'd shut her out.

Her heart plummeted. She pulled her hands through her hair, desolation emptying into her like smoke into a black void.

What had she just thrown away?

05:45 Charlie, Venturion Tower, Manhattan, Sunday, October 5

Samuel Killinger stood at the head of the table and addressed his board via a plasma screen. "I've just received word from our Nexus team that a full-scale revolution is breaking out in Hamān. The rightful heir to the kingdom has apparently returned, and the majority of Hamānians are seeing this as some sort of sign to take up arms and rise against the monarchy. The place is about to spiral out of control."

"We're evacuating the compound?"

"As we speak. We've initiated emergency procedures and are destroying any biological material that might implicate us should the country fall. But this will not, and I repeat, *not,* impact our plans. This is just one of the risks that comes hand in hand with the benefits of doing business in a country like Hamān. It's nothing we're not prepared to handle."

He paused. "And the pathogen is ready be released at a moment's notice. The antidote stockpiles are in place offshore, and you all have vials of your own. We're good to go."

He leaned forward, hands on the table. "I trust that the next time we meet, it will be to watch President Elliot resign—" he smiled "—in eight days. Good night, gentlemen."

Killinger closed the meeting and retired to his office. He was going to forget his hit man and Dr. Sterling for now.

If they were still alive, they were going to be ensnared in civil unrest for God knew how long.

By the time things leveled out in Hamān—if ever— Grayson Forbes would be the new U.S. President and nothing would—*could*—touch him.

Or Olivia.

The Nexus compound would no longer exist. The labs and computer system would have been destroyed. And his assassin, if he found his way out alive, could never be linked to him.

And if—just *if*—Dr. Paige Sterling was still alive and rattling around somewhere in that archaic country, she was going to be of no use to anyone. Any information that eventually came out of her was going to be too little—and too late.

06:02 Charlie, Asir Mountains, Sunday, October 5

A precipitous trail unfurled below them, dry, hot and twisting between large sand-gold boulders and rocks. Even at this early hour the fierceness of the sun was unrelenting.

Rafiq halted his camel, wiped beads of perspiration from his forehead, lifted his binoculars and surveyed the terrain below. There were troops massing on *both* sides of the Hamāni and the Saudi border now.

He scanned slowly toward the south, to where monstrous coils of black razor wire ran the length of the desert down to the coast—the Yemeni border.

He moved his scopes along the length of the wire. There was mobilization on the Yemeni front, too. He could detect movement in the watchtowers that punctuated the coils of wire.

He lowered his scopes. It looked as if Hamān's not-so-friendly neighbors could smell trouble brewing in the country, and it was making them nervous. He could use this to divert attention from himself and Paige when they made a run for the coast tonight.

He raised the scopes to his eyes again. There was a blur of fine sand blowing low across the plains. Could be signs of a sandstorm coming. He could use that, too. If it picked up, it could get brutal, but it would hide their approach.

"We need to get down there," he said, pointing to the black strip of razor wire which could be seen from their vantage point. "That's the Yemeni front. We wait over there." He pointed to a rise of dunes about three hundred yards out from the Yemeni border. "We lie low behind that ridge until nightfall. Then we make a run for the ocean about three miles that way."

"How? They'll see us."

"I'll figure that out when we get there," he said, his words clipped. He nudged his camel forward without looking at her. If he did, her eyes would suck him in again. He didn't want that. He wanted his head clear. He wasn't going to think about anything other than getting her out and onto that boat tonight.

And *then* he'd show her who stuck to his promises.

"Rafiq, wait…please."

He stopped. But he refused to turn around.

"Rafiq, please, look at me."

He didn't. The muscles in his neck bunched tight.

"I…I need to explain…I'm just—"

"Just what!" He whirled round to face her. "Incapable of faith? Can you not find it in yourself to *trust* me?"

She recoiled visibly. "This…this is not about trust."

"Damn right, it is."

"No, it's not! It's…it's because I learned the hard way what waiting for someone can do to you—waiting and waiting for someone you love who's never coming back. I just can't do it." Emotion ripped through her voice, driving it higher. "I can't set myself up to be let down again."

Someone you love? Rafiq's eyes began to burn. In this short life-and-death time together, she'd developed feelings for him as strong as his were for her. And she was too damn afraid to admit it, to accept it, to embrace it. *That's* what this was about.

"Paige," he said gently, turning his camel about and bringing it up against hers. "This *is* about trust. It's about letting go and having absolute faith in someone else, in believing that they *will* be there for you—if you let them."

Her eyes swam with moisture and she began to shake. Paige knew he was asking her to have faith in him. But faith had damn near destroyed her as a kid. And it was useless in her line of work. She dealt with facts. And the fact she might never see Rafiq after today was a very real possibility.

He might not even survive.

Besides, even if he did, he had a path to take that was very different from hers. If he managed to reclaim his country, he was going to have to think long and hard about what kind of woman—or *women*—he needed by his side, and what message his choice would send to his subjects and his international allies. She might not fit the bill.

She might just be indicted. Labeled a criminal. Sent to prison.

So why set herself up for emotional destruction? She'd never indulged in fairy tales and dreams of princesses and knights and warrior kings in exotic lands. Why now?

He reached for her hand. "You're afraid, Paige. I think you actually have a *pathological* fear of commitment."

So what if she did? The knowledge didn't make her any more able to handle it. She pulled her hand away.

Hurt welled in his eyes. "Paige, we have something special here." He paused, his eyes watching hers. "I've never been with a woman in the way I was with you. You do know that, don't you?"

A ball swelled in her throat. She did know it. "It was the stress, the adrenaline, Rafiq. Humans do these things under those kinds of situations. It's a purely physiological response."

He reeled visibly.

She looked away. "Humans do odd things under pressure. They…say things they might regret later."

His eyes crackled with anger. "I do *not* play games, Dr. Sterling," he growled. "I'm an all-or-nothing kind of guy. I've had plenty women in my life but never have I misled a single one of them about my intentions. *Ever!* And only twice in my life have I loved. Both times it happened fast." He waited her for to look back into his eyes. "And it looks like both times I get to lose."

He whirled his camel round in a cloud of dust.

Paige watched him go down the mountain, feeling as if she'd just been punched.

Chapter 15

Rafiq swore violently as he negotiated the steep trail, passionate anger and emotions roiling inside him. He clenched his teeth as his camel slipped sideways. He righted the animal.

He was going to have to hold his passion in check, at least until Paige was safe. But there was no way *he* could lock his feelings away again. The genie was out of the bottle. All he could do was ride his passions out, control them the way he would a belligerent camel.

And deal with her later.

Hot wind whipped the assassin's robes as he scanned the Asir Mountains through binoculars. He was waiting down near the Saudi border where the Hamānian army expected Rafiq to cross. And he knew for certain the woman—his target—was with Rafiq. The hunter had told them so. But they'd lost them in the monsoon last night, and the trigger-happy militia fools had shot the hunter dead before they could use his dogs to resume the trace in the morning.

So the troops had come down here, to the border, instead. To wait for them.

He slowly panned the southern escarpment. If it were him, *that's* where he'd cross, in the south where the Hamānians least expected him to. And from there he'd head through Yemen down to the Gulf of Aden, which was free of Hamānian navy patrols. He studied the terrain inch by inch, the glare making his pale eyes hurt.

Then he saw something—a quick glint of sunlight on metal.

He stilled, stared intently at the spot, his eyes watering, the wind irritating.

He concentrated on closing out physical sensation.

Through his scopes he saw a wisp of dust separate from the dun-colored mountain terrain and eddy up the flanks in the rising wind. Was that human movement? He couldn't be sure, his eyes were beginning to blur.

He lowered the binoculars, rubbed his eyes, put his shades back on. The glint and the wisp of dust could have been anything—the sun on a shard of old glass, an animal making a kill.

But his gut told him different.

He was done with these military fools. Their purpose had been served. He covered his face with his turban, sidled to the outskirts of the troops, and slipped off into the sand-filled wind.

He had a job to finish, a call to place to Manhattan, and a check to collect.

19:37 Charlie, Hamān-Yemen border, Sunday, October 5

The sandstorm blew fierce, and it blew for hours, carrying sand from miles across the Rub Al-Khali and lashing it at the troops huddling along the fronts. It tore at armored vehicles, wobbled jeeps, jammed weapons with grit and forced fine yellow grains into the pores of any bit of skin left exposed.

Paige huddled against Rafiq as sand piled up on them in back-eddy drifts. For the first time, she was truly grateful for the *chador.* But even under the tent of fabric, sand caked her lashes and filled her mouth with grit.

Rafiq had set the camels free in the foothills, taking only the weapons and water. They'd hunched over and run low, right into the grating teeth of the wind, until they'd reached a ridge of dunes. No one had seen them, and they'd been pressed up against the leeward side of the dunes, a wave of sand howling over their heads since noon.

It was now dark. Her joints were stiff, her muscles ached, her lips were dry and cracked, and the constant moaning in the wind was making her feel edgy.

She'd lost track of time once darkness had fallen, and she had no idea what hour it was when the wind finally began to abate.

Rafiq lifted his head and shook sand from his tunic. She moved slowly, blinking, her eyes sore and watering. While wind still rushed over the plain with a soft rustling hiss, it was now protected and calm in the lee of their dune, and the terrible moaning had stopped. She shook out her *chador,* and saw that the sky above was clear.

Rafiq pushed a canteen of water into her hands and Paige drank gratefully, each swallow painful against the rawness in her throat. She wiped her mouth, the movement scratching sand across her sensitive skin. She winced, handed the canteen back to him.

He took a sip, replaced the cap. "Wait here." His words were clipped. He was still angry with her.

"Where are you going?" she whispered nervously.

"I need to get close to that watchtower on the other side of this ridge before the wind dies completely. The sand will provide some cover."

Her chest tightened. "What if they see you?"

He hesitated. "If I'm not back in thirty minutes, do *not* wait. No matter what's happening, get low and run down to the sea." He pushed his satellite phone into her hands. "Here. It's got a clock. It's got GPS. They'll know where you are. When you get down to the estuary, press 99. That will give them the signal you're ready for evacuation."

Panic nipped at her. "Rafiq—"

"You'll be fine."

She grabbed his hand, held him back. "Rafiq, do you see what you're doing?" she whispered urgently. "You're preparing for not coming back. *See?*" Her eyes felt hot. "All that stuff about faith and trust—it's bogus."

He was quiet for a second. "Do you always have to be *so* goddamn logical, Dr. Sterling?"

"Practical," she hissed at him. "Realistic."

"Irritating," he growled, leaning close to her, his breath brushing over her lips. "And I'll tell you what's not practical—having this argument *now*."

"Well, I'm not going to wait—"

"Damn right you're not. You're going to get your ass down to that ocean."

And he was gone.

She flopped her head back against the sand, her heart beating hard against her ribs. "Damn you, Rafiq," she whispered angrily up to the stars. "You better get your *own* ass back here."

Rafiq belly-crawled along the sand until he was well within a hundred yards of his target.

He brought the mounted rifle scope to his eye, thankful that the weapon in his hands was an AK—designed to function in the worst of crap, including sand. Its drawback was the sound, but the howling wind would mask the direction from which his shot came.

He squinted into the wind, his lashes thick with sand. He waiting until his target came into view, his heart beating steady, his breathing controlled, his finger relaxed on the trigger. The Hamānian rifleman came around the side of the jeep and entered his crosshairs. Rafiq aimed just beyond the man's shoulder and fired.

The Hamānian froze for a split second as the bullet whizzed past him, and in that time Rafiq targeted a Yemeni guard up in the watchtower on the other side of the border. He squeezed the trigger and the guard reeled as bullets flew past his shoulder. Someone screamed.

Rafiq immediately fired on the Hamānians again, letting loose a shower of bullets that pinged against their armored cars. Then his luck hit—a gas tank exploded in a whoosh of violent flame.

Hamānians were now blindly firing on the Yemenis, and Yemeni soldiers returned the shots. Gunfire peppered the air, and there was yelling as panic and full-scale battle erupted. Flashlights burst from the watch turrets and began to pan the desert. More gunfire sounded over the wind as the border skirmish spread north and engaged the Saudi troops.

Mission accomplished. Rafiq hoped there would be no serious casualties, but this was the *only* way to get Paige out unnoticed.

He squirmed back over the sand, found Paige huddled against the dune, eyes wide as saucers in the dark.

"Thank God you—"

"Come," he hissed, grabbing her hand.

They hunkered down and ran low, parallel to the razor wire, two black ghosts making for the tidal estuary as all military power was focused on the chaos to the north.

The estuary was only about three miles from their dune hideout, but sand had piled into soft drifts. Paige stumbled under the weight of her heavy cloth. She was tired, breathing hard. Rafiq slowed a little, giving her time. They could afford the luxury—they were in the clear, and they were going to make it.

They reached a mangrove swamp and immediately Rafiq could feel the increase in humidity. And once in the protection of dense vegetation, there was no wind. The combination of moisture and hot hair produced a low swirling fog over the black surface of the water, and a strange, sudden silence. The thin light of the moon made the fog glow eerily.

He pulled Paige down to his side. "Give me the phone," he whispered.

She handed it to him and he punched in the code. Two seconds later, a light flashed once out at sea.

"They're out there," he whispered, giving her hand a squeeze.

He drew her into the silty water, warm and soft as velvet. They crouched down into the reeds and mangrove shrubs, shrouded in the fog. The tide was low and the moonlight made strange shadows of open root systems. But it was *too* quiet, the stillness too dense, and somehow ominous. There *should* be night noise in a swamp like this. He didn't like it.

Paige was uneasy, too, he could sense it. She glanced sideways at him, her eyes glinting. "I feel like we're being watched," she whispered very softly.

He did, too. But he didn't say so. "Can you swim?" he kept his voice real low.

"Yes," she whispered. "But not in these clothes. They'll weigh me down like a rock."

Something scuttled suddenly in the branches. Paige gasped, turned slightly, making a soft splash; a startled bird took flight. Then all was deathly still again, as if the mangrove trees were closing in on them, strangling out sound.

He had a real bad feeling about this. He took her hand. "We're going to wade out to meet the inflatable. Right now those black clothes are cover, but if we need to swim, shed the gear, okay? And swim in the direction of that flash of light you just saw. Hold the orientation in your mind."

Water sloshed softly around them as they moved deeper. Then he saw it, a tiny pinprick of light, followed the gentle slap and swish of oars. A dark silhouette took shape on the water.

December. His pulse kicked into gear.

They waited, thigh deep in the water, as the small dinghy came closer. December was as black as night. All Rafiq could see was the massiveness of his silhouette, the whites of his eyes, and the glint of his teeth.

The inflatable drew up to them. "Hey, Zayed."

"December, good to see you." He handed Paige over to him. But just as he did, a single shot cracked through the fog.

They froze.

Another shot slammed into the water, splashing it up into Rafiq's face.

He cursed and shoved Paige into the dinghy. "Get her to the boat," he hissed. "Now!"

He turned, fired into the blackness, sunk down into the water, watching the darkness. That was no Hamānian soldier firing on them. This appeared to be a lone sniper—a sharpshooter who'd kept his eye on them, tracked them all the way down to the swamp. Or worse, anticipated their coming here.

The hair on the back of his neck rose; the hunter was being hunted.

Who, goddammit? Who could have been tracking them?

Rafiq fired blindly into the dark, trying to buy December time to get Paige behind the line of trees and out into open water.

The sniper fired again. Rafiq heard December grunt sharply in the distance.

He'd been hit.

Rage mushroomed inside him, and fear for Paige. But the splash of paddles continued. December was still moving. He forced calm on himself. He had a direction for the shooter now. He aimed and fired—again and again and again—until the little inflatable disappeared from view behind the low dense trees and out into the open waters of the Gulf of Aden.

Relief ebbed through him, and his heart grew hard and steady. He was going to find this bastard. But he had to take him alive, find out who the hell he was, who he was working for. Because if this sniper was linked to the Cabal…

Rafiq edged farther into the reeds, beginning to work his way around back in the direction he believed the shots had come from. And he prayed December was okay, that he'd get Paige onto the fishing boat, that he'd make it back to help him capture this stalker.

He edged out of the water, clothes dripping, the small plops on the surface giving away his location. It made him nervous. And that ate at him. He didn't do nervous. This was something new to him.

He circled round, uneasily aware that someone out there might be circling back on him.

Then he saw him.

A hulking shadow of a figure, covered in black with a black headcloth wound around his head. He had his back to Rafiq, his rifle resting in the crook of two twisted mangrove branches. The man was panning the estuary, *looking for him.*

Then the man moved sharply to his left. He'd spotted December in the inflatable, heading back for him.

The man slowly lowered his eye to his rifle.

Rafiq's chest went tight. He quietly reached for his *jambiya,* unsheathed it as he crept toward the figure.

The man now had his sights trained on December's silhouette and was following him as he moved between the trees, through the swirling fog. He was going for a kill shot. Rafiq raised his arm and flung the dagger with a sharp flick of his wrist.

The man seemed to sense it coming. He bolted up, spun round, his rifle aimed out from his stomach. But before he could jerk back on the trigger, the *jambiya* sank into his neck at the shoulder.

He squeezed the trigger as his knees gave out under him,

the shots going wild. The man dropped the gun and his hands came up to grab the dagger sticking out of his neck. Rafiq drew his scimitar, decades of anger and the ferocity of his ancestors suddenly surging through his blood. He lunged with his sword.

But the man had the reactions and sixth sense of a trained warrior. He moved sideways and Rafiq's sword met air, throwing him off balance.

The man came back at him, lurching with his full weight, dagger still protruding from his neck, and the sheer force of his momentum and mass took Rafiq down to the ground with a thud. They grappled in the roots and swamp muck. The man's strength was inhuman, even with a knife in his neck and blood pumping from his wound, he managed to wrestle Rafiq into the ground, but Rafiq reached up, clasped his hands behind the man's neck, closed his eyes tight, and yanked the man down into a smashing head butt. It temporarily disoriented him and Rafiq pulled him down again, slamming his shoulder against the hilt of the dagger.

The man screamed in pain as the blade was forced deeper, but he came right back up as Rafiq tried to roll away, catching himself in a mangrove root. The man raised a boot over his head and Rafiq noted in some distant part of his brain that the man was wearing gloves.

But just before he brought the boot down, a shot cracked the air. *December!*

The man's body shuddered, and his eyes went wide, glowing strangely surreal in the moonlight. Then he crumpled into a heap, groaning in pain, clutching his chest as blood glistened over his black gloves.

Rafiq glanced at December coming toward him, doubled over in pain, holding his gun in one hand, clutching the side of his belly with the other. He'd been shot in the gut. This was not good.

Rafiq scrambled to his feet, groped for his scimitar, pushed the man onto his back and pinned him there with his knees. "Move and I kill you, jackass."

He reached down, and ripped off the man's turban. Shock rippled through him. The man was as pale as a ghost in the moonlight, his hair a close-cropped shock of luminous white. December came to his side, still doubled over. He shone a small flashlight into the man's face. The sniper's eyes glowed red. Rafiq jerked back in surprise. "Who the hell are you?" he growled.

Silence. Just the glow of red eyes. It was damned unnerving.

Rafiq shot a look at December, who was hunched over in pain. Blood, or water, or both, saturated his shirt. "Can you make it back?"

"I'll live…let's…get this bastard out of here. We'll need to squeeze him. Is he alone?"

Rafiq could hear an uncharacteristic catch in his buddy's bass voice. Doubt and urgency spurted through him. "As far as I can see." Rafiq quickly patted the guy down, could find no communication device. Unusual. But at least it meant no external contact with anyone who could alert the Cabal, which in turn could set off the bombs. That was a good thing. But if he was somehow linked to the Cabal, how the hell had Snow White here gotten into Hamān? What was he doing down at the estuary while the place was swarming with military? This man had to have connections, high up. To the palace. To Sadiq.

They had to get him out and fast, before news of this could travel.

* * *

23:14 Charlie, Gulf of Aden, Sunday, October 5

Paige stood at the prow of the old fishing boat, waves slapping softly at the hull. December had been rushed into the cabin and was being treated by one of the FDS soldiers on board, a big guy with an Irish accent named Hunter McBride. He appeared to be some kind of doctor. The albino was bound and bleeding down in the hold.

She felt sick.

Rafiq came up behind her, touched her shoulders, turned her around to face him. Light from a lantern in the cabin threw his face into a blend of warm and stark shadow.

She touched his forehead with her fingertips. "Your skin is cut, you're bleeding."

His eyes lanced hers, and he said nothing.

Tension wound her stomach tight. "You're…going back now, aren't you."

He nodded.

And for the first time, she honestly didn't want him to. She felt selfish enough to want him all to herself. She wanted to run off with him—away from all this responsibility.

She hugged herself. She knew what she was up against, knew she'd probably never see him again. "I don't want you to go," she whispered, her eyes growing hot with emotion.

He pulled her hard up against his body, pressed his mouth over hers in a kiss as passionate and powerful as life itself. Tears streamed down her cheeks as she melted into him, held him, kissed him. And she knew she was done for. Because despite her fears, she *was* going to wait…for someone she loved to come back.

He pulled back, cupped her face, looked into her eyes. And she realized his own were filled with emotion. "Go do your thing in that lab, Doctor," he said in a cracked, thick voice. "They *need* you."

And his people needed him.

He swallowed. "Paige, I'll be back. I—"

She shook her head, pressed her fingers over his lips. "Don't say it, please."

He nodded.

And Paige tried to hold down the most sharp and painful ball of emotion she'd ever felt in her life. "Go," she said, her voice hoarse. "Now."

Paige stood at the stern as engines began to rumble in the bowels of the boat and white water churned in the moonlight.

She watched his dinghy disappear into the shadow and mist of the mangrove swamp, taking her heart and soul with him.

"Be safe, Rafiq bin Zafir bin Omar al-Qaadr," she whispered. "Come back to me someday."

But she knew he wouldn't, couldn't.

She wiped her eyes, the salty tears burning her skin.

Why, Paige, why a bloody *sultan?* Why fall for a man you can never have?

"Dr. Sterling?" She jumped at the voice and spun around. It was Hunter McBride.

He touched her shoulder. "You okay?"

His touch was so firm and yet so gentle, a healer's hands. This was one of the guys Rafiq had said he trusted with his life. One of his mates. Tears blurred her vision.

Hunter held out a tissue. "Chopper's on its way, Doctor."

She took the tissue, wiped her face, sniffed. "Thank

you. I'm fine, really." She cleared her throat, pulling herself together.

She, too, had a job to do.

Chapter 16

Rafiq galloped over the plains toward Na'jif as the rising sun turned the dust-laden sky brilliant red. His black stallion snorted heavily, its coat glistening from exertion. Rafiq, too, was drenched beneath his robes, his throat dry with thirst.

He'd taken the horse and supplies from Hamānian troops at the Yemeni border, the skirmish providing cover. He'd ridden hard and fast through the night, making short work of the pass.

Within a few hours he and the carpet dealer would be coordinating the troops of the Silent Revolution. If luck and destiny prevailed, Al Qatar could fall by midnight.

And he would be king.

* * *

23:21 Alpha, São Diogo Island, Tuesday, October 7

Paige hadn't slept at all since she'd arrived on São Diogo two days ago. She'd been working round the clock in the Level 4 lab with Meyer and the medical team, analyzing the research data from the Nexus system and directing the manufacture of the antidote.

Meanwhile, the techs had managed to locate information in the Nexus system that showed where the Cabal had hidden its own antidote stockpiles, and FDS troops were ready to move on the offshore locations if the biological bombs were released. But they couldn't act a minute sooner—it would tip the Cabal and trigger the bombs. They had to manufacture what they could on São Diogo.

Jacques Sauvage himself had departed earlier in the day for New York to hunt down Samuel Killinger on his home ground. Killinger, Paige had been told, was head of the Venturion Corporation board, and leader of the Cabal. But the FDS couldn't just move in and take him down overtly, because that too would trigger the release of the pathogen.

Killinger had to be taken by stealth and he had to be forced to pull the plug on the bombs himself. Paige had been told that Sauvage alone knew how to make him do that.

She checked her watch as she walked along the deserted corridor toward the cafeteria, mentally calculating the time difference in New York. Sauvage had seven days to stop the Cabal and save the United States government. She pushed open the door to the empty cafeteria, flicked on the neon lights, wondering if he'd manage to do it in time.

She prayed he had a better shot at succeeding than she'd had of saving the president.

She'd learned from the Q3 systems what variation of the

pathogen had been given to President Elliot and how it
worked. And she'd developed an antidote. It was decep-
tively simple, but it was too late. Even if it were possible
to administer the antidote immediately, Elliot still wouldn't
make it. His brain was already too damaged.

The harsh neon lights flickered overhead as Paige made
for the pot of coffee. She poured a cup of the thick brew
and seated herself at a table near the window. It was dark
outside and her reflection was stark against the black
window. She turned her chair away from it not wanting to
look at herself in this exhausted condition.

She was still wearing scrubs. Her hair was scraped back
into a tight ponytail and her complexion was wan. She'd
lost a little weight since she'd been kidnapped almost a
week ago. But she didn't want to think about food.

She cupped her mug in both hands, sipped slowly. All
of this had happened because of her parents and their discovery. Paige wondered how different things might have
been if her dad had not chickened out that day in Brussels,
if he *had* told Meyer all those years ago that he believed
the rare prion disease in the bonobo troop was caused by
spiroplasma and not prions themselves.

She'd gone on to prove it, and that in turn meant it
was curable. Because spiroplasma—small bacteria
without cell walls that were present in the hemolymph
of almost all insects—were sensitive to broad-spectrum
antibiotics.

That meant many variations of transmissible spongiform encephalopathies—or prion diseases—could be
cured, but only if the antidote was given at the very earliest
stages of the disease. Otherwise, the hosts' brains would
be irreparably damaged.

And that was the case with President Elliot. She set her mug down, dropped her face into her hands.

Meyer had said her work was genius but she felt like a complete failure. Tears began once again to well in her eyes. This was ridiculous. For the better part of her adult life she'd hardly ever cried. Now she couldn't stop.

She wiped the moisture from her eyes in frustration and looked up at the television screen mounted in the far corner of the cafeteria. She wanted to know what was happening in the Middle East, but at the same time she couldn't bear seeing any more news of Hamān or any more images of the "handsome and mysterious Sultan" who'd returned to bring down Sadiq's regime, tumbling the entire region into turmoil virtually overnight.

Rafiq had ridden into Al Qatar on the morning of the sixth with the armies of the Silent Revolution at his flanks. They must have been a frightening sight, racing over the desert toward the walled capital, sand boiling in their wake.

The instant he'd publicly declared his return to Hamān, the Royal Hamānian military forces had collapsed, with thousands of defectors rushing to join the highly-coordinated Silent Revolution. And in less than twenty-four hours, the capital had fallen.

Sadiq and a handful of loyalists had barricaded themselves in the palace compound. According to the last news report Paige had seen, the infamous 'Scarred Sultan' was now trying to negotiate his life in exchange for handover to an international tribunal.

The gates to freedom and democracy in Hamān were officially open, but according to reporters, the real battle for the new Sultan Rafiq bin Zafir bin Omar al-Qaadr still lay ahead. Rebuilding his country and opening it to trade with the Western world would take decades. And he was there, serving his people, doing his job.

And she was here doing hers.

Paige stared at the pattern on the melamine table. She felt hollow, left out. Cold. Her work had always fulfilled her. She'd never minded being on the outside, an observer.

But she did now.

There was a hot, vibrant and passionate world out there. And she was here, once again, by herself. And right now, in her exhausted state, she was sorry she'd ever met Rafiq, because now nothing in her life could ever match up to him.

Another delinquent tear escaped her eye. It slid down her cheek, dangled from her chin and fell with a plop into her coffee. But Paige didn't care enough to wipe them away anymore.

Rafiq stood in the dark hallway, looking in at the brightly lit cafeteria, watching Paige. His heart ached with a pain so deep he could barely breathe. She looked so sad, so tired. So broken.

He sucked in a deep breath, trying to find courage for what he'd come to do. Almost a week ago he'd been just like this, out in the dark, looking in at her, knowing that somehow Paige Sterling held all the answers.

He'd come to take her again. But this time he wanted her to come of her own volition. It was the final test. And Rafiq was afraid—that she'd say no.

He was more afraid of her rejection than anything else he'd ever experienced. When he'd taken her from that lab in Hamān, the global stakes had been high. Now it was his heart on the line.

He clenched and unclenched his fists at his sides. He

didn't have much time. He shouldn't even be here. The jet was still fueled, waiting. He had to move. Now.

He made his way to the cafeteria entrance, stood quietly in the doorway. She was staring up at the blank television screen.

"Would you like me to turn that on for you?"

She spun round and froze.

"Hello, Doctor." He smiled, but his heart was hammering hard, his palms damp.

Her mouth dropped open and her eyes went huge. She stood, knocking over her chair. *"Rafiq?"*

He held his hands out to his side. "Surprised?"

Her eyes flicked to the blank screen, then back to him. "You…you're supposed to be—"

He cocked a brow, smiled again. "On TV?"

"No, I mean…you were in Hamān, on the news. You…all the networks are going crazy, there's coverage all the time."

"Can you blame them?" he said, stepping into the room. "It's the first time the country has *ever* been open to the media. The place is flooding with journalists."

He took another step toward her and she tensed visibly. "What…what are you doing here?" She put her hand to her forehead, as if she was afraid she was hallucinating. "You *can't* be here. You…the palace…Al Qatar has just fallen…you have…"

The nerves in his chest squeezed tighter. His smiled faded. "I'm not staying, Paige."

She swallowed sharply, and her hands dropped to her sides.

He took another step toward her. "Paige, I have a jet waiting—"

She lifted both hands, stopping him in his tracks. "Look,

if you've come to say goodbye, I…I'd rather you hadn't, Rafiq. I'd rather you turned around right now, walked out that door. Because…if…if you touch me…" Her voice cracked and she reached for the back of a chair.

He didn't listen. He kept walking, coming right up to her. Paige closed her eyes, unable to bear the emotions overwhelming her. She willed him to turn around and leave, and she willed him to grab her, hold her, kiss her, never let her go.

He came nearer. She still couldn't open her eyes. She could smell him, that faint exotic scent of the deserts of Hamān. She could feel his warmth. Her chest twisted so tightly she thought her heart might literally break.

If she looked at him now…saw the way his hair fell glossy and loose to the shoulders of his crisp white shirt, the way his skin was tanned even darker from days under the sun, the way his eyes gleamed as if they held the answer to life itself, the way his jeans moved like sin over his hips, the way he wore those black leather boots. The way his scimitar rested against his thigh.

Paige tried to swallow, and tears squeezed out from under her lashes. But she could *not* look at him.

"Paige?"

She felt his fingers touch her jaw bone, and a small sound escaped her chest.

"Look at me, Paige."

"Please, Rafiq, say goodbye. Get it over with. Don't do this to me."

"*Paige,*" he said firmly, and his lips brushed softly over hers. Her knees went weak and her hands began to shake.

"I didn't come to say goodbye," he whispered over her mouth.

Her eyes flared open. "Why *did* you come, then?"

"Because I made a date. I made a promise. And—" he lifted her chin with his knuckle "—I *always* keep my promises. I had no intention of making you wait—" he hesitated, a flicker of nerves in his eyes "—for someone you love."

She couldn't speak.

That glimmer of unease deepened in his oil-black eyes. "You…did mean it, Paige…didn't you?"

She didn't trust herself to make a sound. All she could do was nod her head.

A small breath of relief escaped him, but the uncertainty lingered in his eyes. "The jet is waiting," he said softly. "I want you come *home* with me, Paige. I want you to be at my side."

She tried to make her brain work. She smudged the tears from her cheeks. "Rafiq, I…I don't understand. I can't go anywhere. I made this pathogen. Authorities will want to speak to me. I—"

His eyes narrowed with hot intensity. "Your work is done here, Paige."

"No, it's not. Whether those bombs go off or not, the President of the United States *is* going to die. And it's my fault—"

He gripped her by the shoulders, his eyes flashing. "No, it is not!"

"It is! You said so yourself, I would be indicted for treason. I—"

He steadied her, forced her look into his eyes. "Paige, you were a pawn, and the FDS will protect you. And I can tell you, no one is going to come after the Queen of Hamān, not on my watch. You will *always* be safe with me."

She felt her jaw drop. "What…did you say?"

He hesitated. "I wanted to do this properly, but there is no time." He paused. "I want you to be my queen, Paige, my *only* queen. And I want you to help guide our country into a democratic future. I want you at my side."

"But—"

He placed his fingers over her mouth, shook his head. "You don't have to say anything now. All you have to do is come home with me. And from there we will take it one day at a time. You can leave Hamān whenever you wish, *if* you wish. But I want you to see if you like it, if you can help me lead my people into a new world." He paused, his eyes searing hers. "Because, Paige, I know you can handle my country. And I know you love my people. And more than anything, I know I love you."

A lump of emotion lodged in her throat. "Rafiq, I'm not of Hamānian blood. I'm not of royal lineage. Your people might not accept me as their queen. Have you thought about that?"

His black eyes glittered and a broad smile cracked his dark face. "You are considering it, then?"

"You're not thinking it through, Rafiq. Choosing me might be sending the wrong signal to your people. It might not be in the interests of peace."

He cupped her face firmly. "Always the thinker, aren't you, Paige? But you are wrong this time. You are my destiny, and you are Hamān's destiny, should you choose to accept me."

He exhaled heavily. "If it wasn't for this mission, Paige, if it wasn't *you* in that lab, working late when you should have been sleeping, I would never have gone back to save my country. You are part of the legend of Hamān. *You* brought their mythical savior home, made him real. My people will see that."

He took her in his arms. "Will you accept me, Paige? Will you come home with me?"

Paige felt as if she'd swallowed pure sunshine. The tears that rolled down her cheeks now were sheer, sweet emotional release.

"Is that a yes?"

She bit her lip, nodded. "Yes," she said in Arabic. It was all she could manage.

He kissed her so hard, so suddenly, so possessively, she couldn't breathe. Her heart thudded against his chest and her limbs melted. His body was so solid. So warm. So *alive*. Paige felt as if she was tasting life itself. And never had she felt more happy—or excited—about a future.

He scooped her off her feet, in her scrubs, and he moved toward the door with powerful, playful ease. "Our jet is waiting."

Paige closed her eyes as he swept her out the door. This could not be happening. Fairy tales could actually come true. There *were* warrior kings and knights in shining armor—even for girls who'd been taught not to believe.

Epilogue

00:02 Alpha, Over the Atlantic, Tuesday, October 7

Jacques Sauvage got the news about three hours before touchdown at JFK. December had come out of surgery and was now in ICU in the São Diogo hospital. His condition was stable but critical. He'd lost massive amounts of blood due to internal bleeding and was barely hanging on with life support.

In the meanwhile, his FDS interrogators were working on the injured sniper they'd captured in Hamān but the strange man wasn't talking. Yet.

Sauvage leaned back in his seat, closed his eyes, the drone of the FDS jet steady in his ears. His techs had also found evidence in the Nexus Q3 systems of an offshore antidote stockpile. If the bioattack was launched, they could move on the stockpiles, save some lives.

Now all he had to do was keep the plague from being spread in the first place. And he had to stop the Cabal from overthrowing the government of the United States. That meant taking the Cabal down at the head before the president made his speech. He had seven days to do it.

And he was going to have to use Olivia.

He was going to have to see her again. Touch her.

Sauvage clenched the armrests, drew in a long, slow, steady breath.

This had just gotten personal—*too personal.*

* * * * *

The SHADOW SOLDIERS *saga continues with*
RULES OF RE-ENGAGEMENT
by Loreth Anne White
The final countdown has begun, and
Jacques Sauvage has only a few days left to
complete his mission. But to achieve his goal,
he will have to confront his past and face the
only woman he ever loved…and lost.
Can he win her heart in time to keep her alive?
Available December 2006,
wherever Silhouette Books are sold.

Dear Reader,

My SHADOW SOLDIERS have gone to extreme lengths to bury their pasts. But while it's one thing to try and escape a deed, can one ever really run from oneself?

This is the conflict faced by Rafiq Zayed, a mercenary who tries to hide the fact that the blood of ancient warrior sheiks pulses in his veins. But, in a bid to stop a global threat of almost incomprehensible proportion, Rafiq is forced to return to the land of his birth. There the man of passionate action clashes with a woman of cool logic, and the past and present and future collide in a mysterious land as old as time. But the clock is ticking, and unless my hero and heroine can confront their own pasts, they will not be able to save their future.

However, it will take more than passion or logic to do it—it will take love.

Loreth Anne White

New York Times *bestselling author*
Linda Lael Miller
is back with a new romance featuring
the heartwarming McKettrick family
from Silhouette Special Edition.

SIERRA'S HOMECOMING
by Linda Lael Miller

On sale December 2006,
wherever Silhouette books are sold.

Turn the page for a sneak preview!

Soft, smoky music poured into the room.

The next thing she knew, Sierra was in Travis's arms, close against that chest she'd admired earlier, and they were slow dancing.

Why didn't she pull away?

"Relax," he said. His breath was warm in her hair.

She giggled, more nervous than amused. What was the matter with her? She was attracted to Travis, had been from the first, and he was clearly attracted to her. They were both adults. Why not enjoy a little slow dancing in a ranch-house kitchen?

Because slow dancing led to other things. She took a step back and felt the counter flush against her lower back. Travis naturally came with her, since they were holding hands and he had one arm around her waist.

Simple physics.

Then he kissed her.

Physics again—this time, not so simple.

"Yikes," she said, when their mouths parted.

He grinned. "Nobody's ever said that after I kissed them."

She felt the heat and substance of his body pressed against hers. "It's going to happen, isn't it?" she heard herself whisper.

"Yep," Travis answered.

"But not tonight," Sierra said on a sigh.

"Probably not," Travis agreed.

"When, then?"

He chuckled, gave her a slow, nibbling kiss. "Tomorrow morning," he said. "After you drop Liam off at school."

"Isn't that…a little…soon?"

"Not soon enough," Travis answered, his voice husky. "Not nearly soon enough."

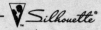

HARLEQUIN® Romance®

From the Heart.
For the Heart.

Get swept away into the Outback with two of Harlequin Romance's top authors.

Coming in December...

Claiming the Cattleman's Heart
BY BARBARA HANNAY

And in January don't miss...

Outback Man Seeks Wife
BY MARGARET WAY

REQUEST YOUR FREE BOOKS!

2 FREE NOVELS
PLUS 2 FREE GIFTS!

Silhouette® Romantic

SUSPENSE

Sparked by Danger, Fueled by Passion!

YES! Please send me 2 FREE Silhouette® Romantic Suspense novels and my 2 FREE gifts. After receiving them, if I don't wish to receive any more books, I can return the shipping statement marked "cancel." If I don't cancel, I will receive 4 brand-new novels every month and be billed just $4.24 per book in the U.S., or $4.99 per book in Canada, plus 25¢ shipping and handling per book plus applicable taxes, if any*. That's a savings of at least 15% off the cover price! I understand that accepting the 2 free books and gifts places me under no obligation to buy anything. I can always return a shipment and cancel at any time. Even if I never buy another book from Silhouette, the two free books and gifts are mine to keep forever.

240 SDN EEX6   340 SDN EEYJ

Name	(PLEASE PRINT)
Address	Apt. #
City	State/Prov.	Zip/Postal Code

Signature (if under 18, a parent or guardian must sign)

Mail to Silhouette Reader Service™:

IN U.S.A.
P.O. Box 1867
Buffalo, NY
14240-1867

IN CANADA
P.O. Box 609
Fort Erie, Ontario
L2A 5X3

Not valid to current Silhouette Intimate Moments subscribers.

Want to try two free books from another line?
Call 1-800-873-8635 or visit www.morefreebooks.com.

* Terms and prices subject to change without notice. NY residents add applicable sales tax. Canadian residents will be charged applicable provincial taxes and GST. This offer is limited to one order per household. All orders subject to approval. Credit or debit balances in a customer's account(s) may be offset by any other outstanding balance owed by or to the customer. Please allow 4 to 6 weeks for delivery.

Harlequin® Historical
Historical Romantic Adventure!

Loyalty...or love?

LORD GREVILLE'S CAPTIVE
Nicola Cornick

He had previously come to Grafton Manor to be betrothed to the beautiful Lady Anne—but that promise was broken with the onset of the English Civil War. Now Lord Greville has returned as an enemy, besieging the manor and holding its lady prisoner.

His devotion to his cause is swayed by his desire for Anne—he will have the lady, and her heart.

Yet Anne has a secret that must be kept from him at all costs....

On sale December 2006.
Available wherever Harlequin books are sold.

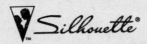Silhouette®

COMING NEXT MONTH

SIMCNM1106

INTIMATE MOMENTS